The Substitute

MARILYN KAYE

BANTAM BOOKS
NEW YORK · TORONTO · LONDON · SYDNEY · AUCKLAND

RL 5.5, 008–012
THE SUBSTITUTE
A Bantam Skylark Book / August 2000

ISBN 0-553-48714-0

Visit us on the Web! www.randomhouse.com/kids

Published simultaneously in the United States and Canada

Bantam Skylark is an imprint of Random House Children's Books, a division of Random House, Inc. SKYLARK BOOK and colophon and BANTAM BOOKS and colophon are registered trademarks of Random House, Inc. Bantam Books, 1540 Broadway, New York, New York 10036.

PRINTED IN THE UNITED STATES OF AMERICA

OPM   10   9   8   7   6   5   4   3   2   1

For my very fine editor
and even finer friend,
Françoise Bui

The Substitute

one

Amy Candler studied the large menu and debated her choices for dinner. Seventh Heaven Heavenly Shrimp sounded pretty good, she thought.

She turned to her best friend, Tasha Morgan, who was sitting alongside her at the round restaurant table. "What are you getting?"

"I can't decide," Tasha said. "It's between the Buffy Bacon Burger and Felicity's Fabulous Fondue."

Tasha's father was frowning. "I don't understand this menu," he grumbled. "South Pork, what's that?"

Amy leaned across the table. "Mom, what are you ordering?"

"I'm thinking about the Popular Pizza," her mother told her. "I guess that must be one of their bestsellers."

Amy and Tasha exchanged exasperated looks. "Mom, it's not called Popular Pizza because it's *popular*," Amy explained patiently. "This is the TV Diner, remember? All the dishes are named after TV shows or the characters on the shows."

"Or TV stars," Tasha added. "Like the Jennifer Love Juice."

Nancy Candler and both the Morgan parents still looked clueless. Amy turned to Eric, who was sitting on her other side. "Do you know what you want?"

Expressionless, Eric shrugged, making a big show of indifference to the whole selection process. "I don't know. Whatever." He glanced back at the menu. "Roswell Chili sounds good."

Tasha read the description. " 'Chili so hot, you'll know it's from another planet.' Eric, you don't like spicy food."

"It does strange things to your stomach," Amy reminded him.

Eric muttered his reply so that only Amy could hear him answer, "Like you care."

Amy said nothing. That was the third snide remark he'd made to her that evening. Tasha hadn't heard him, but she was aware of the tension between her brother and Amy. And she knew what it was all about.

She made an effort to change the subject. "I like your necklace—it's very cool," she told Amy.

Amy fingered the black beads. "Thanks. I found it at a flea market in Paris." Even without looking, she knew that Eric's face had darkened. But what was she supposed to do, never mention Paris again?

She certainly couldn't avoid the subject that evening. That was why the two families had come together for dinner. They were celebrating the return of Amy and her mother from Paris, France. Mr. Morgan wanted to hear about the food they had eaten, the city's architecture, and the historical sites they'd seen. Mrs. Morgan was interested in art and other cultural stuff.

Tasha didn't have many questions, mainly because Amy had already filled her in the night before, when she'd stayed overnight at the Morgans'. Amy had reported on all the really dramatic happenings, the events the Morgan parents—and even Amy's own mother—would never know. Eric knew about Amy's secret adventures too. That was why he was in such a foul mood.

Paris was momentarily forgotten as the waiter appeared to take their orders. "Tell me about this Ally McVeal," Mr. Morgan said to the waiter. "And what is Dawson's Creek Trout?"

Ordering took up some time, but as soon as the waiter left, the topic returned to Paris. "Did you see the view of the city from the top of the Eiffel Tower?" Mrs. Morgan wanted to know.

"Oh, yes," Nancy assured her. "It was spectacular."

Amy tried not to look at Eric, but she could feel the chill of his glare. He didn't mind that she'd been at the top of the Eiffel Tower. He was angry about who she'd been there *with*.

Tasha intercepted the look and moved in to change the subject. "I forgot to tell you last night about the big news at school," she said. "You missed some real excitement."

"Really?" Amy asked. "What happened?"

"Three cheerleaders were kicked off the squad."

"You're kidding!" That *was* news. Being a cheerleader at Parkside Middle School was a very big deal. "Which ones?"

"Amber Vincent, Kristy Diamond, and Vickie Gilligan," Tasha recited. "It turned out they were involved in some scheme to steal the midterm exams."

"Wow," Amy breathed. She wasn't particularly upset by the news, since she didn't even know the three girls, except by reputation. The cheerleaders were all from the most elite clique at Parkside. "What a scandal!" she added.

Tasha nodded. "I was assigned to write the article for

the *Snooze*," she said proudly. That was what everyone called the school newspaper, which was really named *The Parkside News*. "I had to interview all the cheerleaders. Naturally, they all said they knew nothing about the scheme."

"Naturally," Amy echoed. "Those girls stick together."

"And they were so stuck-up," Tasha continued. "I don't know why they think they're so hot."

"Because they are." Eric spoke up. "That Katie Moore is a babe."

Amy had to bite her tongue. She hated to hear any girl referred to as a babe, even a snotty cheerleader. It was so demeaning to females in general.

Eric wasn't usually sexist like that. He probably thought he could make Amy jealous by demonstrating his admiration for another girl's looks. Boys could be so transparent.

"There are going to be open tryouts for girls to replace the cheerleaders," Tasha said.

Mrs. Morgan smiled wistfully. "I always wanted to be a cheerleader when I was in school, but I never made it. You girls should try out."

"What's the point?" Amy asked. "Only girls from that clique ever make it onto the squad. Even if they can't do the moves. The cocaptains make sure of it."

"Oh, that can't be true," her mother objected. "Surely they want the cheerleading team to do well. They wouldn't let an unqualified girl on the team, even if she was one of their friends."

Amy and Tasha exchanged knowing looks. Parents could be so naïve. But Tasha had a surprise for all of them.

"Actually, I *am* thinking about trying out."

Amy blinked. "You are?"

"Sure, why not? I can do pretty decent cartwheels and splits."

"I know you can," Amy replied, "but do you *want* to?" She was totally bewildered. Tasha had never before expressed any interest in cheerleading.

"Not really," Tasha said. "But I just hate the way no one bothers to try out unless they're in that clique. At least maybe I can make some waves. It could turn into a good article for the *Snooze*."

Now Amy understood. It *was* frustrating the way certain cliques controlled certain activities. "Yeah, that's cool. I'll help you practice if you want."

"Great, thanks."

"Amy, why don't you try out too?" Mrs. Morgan asked.

Amy didn't have to look at her own mother to know there was a cautionary expression on her face. There was no way Amy could go out for cheerleading, and Amy knew it.

But she didn't have to answer Mrs. Morgan. Eric did that for her. "Amy can't go out for cheerleading. She'd have to attend all the basketball games, and people might think she cared about one of the players." Eric was on the basketball team. And there was no mistaking the sarcasm in his voice.

It was the harshest—and loudest—comment he'd made, and his mother looked at him in shock. "Eric! What's that supposed to mean?"

"He's just teasing, Mom," Tasha said hastily. "Oh look, here comes our food."

The arrival of dinner distracted everyone, and soon they were all occupied with eating and drinking and trying to figure out the relationship between their food and the TV show it was named for. But Amy couldn't enjoy her Seventh Heaven Heavenly Shrimp. Even if Eric wasn't looking at her, she was all too aware of how he was feeling.

"Excuse me," she murmured midmeal, and left the table. In the rest room, she splashed some water on her face. How long was Eric going to act like this? She knew she shouldn't have told him everything that happened in Paris, but if she hadn't, she would have been keeping secrets from him. And that was no good either.

She slapped more water on her cheeks and left the rest room before anyone could come looking for her.

On her way back to the table, she spotted a familiar face she hadn't noticed on her way to the rest room. "Ms. Weller, hi!"

Her homeroom and English teacher looked up and smiled. "Hello, Amy! How was your trip to Paris?"

"Great," Amy told her. "And very educational," she added quickly, so Ms. Weller wouldn't think she'd missed a week of class for a holiday.

Ms. Weller's companion smiled. "Paris," he sighed. "That's my favorite city in the world."

"I've never been there," Ms. Weller commented. "Dan, I'd like to introduce one of my students, Amy Candler. Amy, this is Dan Lasky."

"How do you do?" Amy said politely, and the man replied with an equally polite "Pleased to meet you, Amy." Then he turned to Ms. Weller. "Maybe we can go to Paris together one day."

Amy could have sworn her teacher's cheeks went a little pinker. She couldn't blame her—Mr. Lasky was very handsome. And from the way he looked into Ms. Weller's eyes, it was clear that something was going on here.

"Well, it was nice running into you, Amy," Ms. Weller said, and Amy realized she had been staring at the two of them.

"Uh, yeah, same here. I'll see you Monday, Ms. Weller."

The teacher nodded and smiled. "See you Monday."

"Goodbye, Mr. Lasky," Amy added.

"Bye, Amy," he said, but he didn't look at her as he spoke. His eyes hadn't left Ms. Weller's face. Amy couldn't wait to get back to her own table now.

"You're not going to believe who I just saw," she reported to Tasha. "Ms. Weller. With a *man*."

"You're kidding!" Tasha squealed. She twisted around in her seat. "Where?"

"Tasha, don't stare," her mother scolded her. "That's very rude."

"I don't see them," Tasha said. "What does the man look like?"

"He's pretty hot," Amy said. "He looks a little like Fox Mulder on *The X-Files*."

"*Wow.*" Tasha squinted. "I still can't see them."

Tasha's father was looking at her. "You've been squinting a lot lately. When was the last time you had your eyes checked?"

"They're holding eye tests at school sometime soon," Mrs. Morgan noted. "I saw an announcement the other day. Tasha, I want you to sign up for that."

"Okay," Tasha murmured, squinting so hard that her whole face wrinkled up.

"I'm sure your mother will want you to take the test too," Mrs. Morgan told Amy. "You girls are right at the age when many people start to need glasses. In fact, I was twelve when I got my first pair. And those tests are free, so you might as well take advantage of it."

"That's a good idea," Nancy Candler said quickly. "Amy, I want you to sign up for the eye exam too."

Amy hid a smile. Her mother knew there wasn't anything wrong with Amy's vision, and there never would be. Tasha was still surveying the room for a glimpse of Ms. Weller and her companion. "Do you think he's her boyfriend?" she asked. "Were they acting as if they were on a date?"

"He likes her, that's for sure," Amy said. "I couldn't tell how she feels. But it definitely wasn't a first date. He was talking about taking her to Paris. Look, they're clinking their glasses together!"

"I can't see!" Tasha complained.

"Girls, stop it!" Nancy said. "You're acting like children. Ms. Weller is entitled to a little privacy on her date. Teachers are people too, you know."

Amy clutched Tasha's arm. "He just kissed her!"

"I want to see!" Tasha wailed.

"I wonder if this is the first big love of her life," Amy

said. "They're looking pretty romantic right now. Just sort of gazing into each other's eyes . . ."

Mr. Morgan sighed. "Ah, the first big love. The one you never forget."

"Yeah," Eric said. "No matter how hard you try."

Amy's shoulders slumped. Clearly, Eric wasn't going to let her off easy anytime soon.

Oh, *why* had she had to open her big fat mouth?

two2

Tasha had an answer for that question later in the evening when the girls were alone in Amy's bedroom.

"You *had* to open your big fat mouth," Tasha said. "Because there was no way you could tell us what happened in Paris without talking about Andy."

"You're right," Amy acknowledged. She flopped down on her bed. "I just didn't expect Eric to get so . . . so . . ." She wasn't sure how to describe the way Eric had reacted to the news that Amy had been with Andy Denker in Paris.

Tasha supplied the right word. "Jealous. Eric's jealous of Andy."

"Did he tell you that?" Amy wanted to know.

"Are you kidding? I'm his sister; he isn't going to tell me anything personal. But it's obvious! He was jealous of Andy back when we were all at Wilderness Adventure together, remember? Andy was stronger than him. He ran faster, he climbed ropes higher, he did everything better than Eric."

"Of course he did," Amy replied. "And Eric knows there's no way he could have competed with Andy. Andy was genetically designed, for crying out loud. He's got a perfect physique. He's superior to other human beings."

"But that's not the only reason Eric was jealous," Tasha pointed out. "He could see how you and Andy were getting along."

Amy was getting exasperated. "Of *course* we got along! Andy is a clone, just like me. We're practically related!"

Tasha snickered. "As I recall, you and Andy weren't exactly behaving like brother and sister back at Wilderness Adventure. I'll bet you didn't act like siblings in Paris, either."

Amy ducked her head to hide a grin. Tasha had

guessed correctly. And Amy hadn't even told her about the kiss she and Andy had shared at the top of the Eiffel Tower.

At least Tasha wasn't angry. "Do you still care about Eric?" she asked.

"Yes. But I care about Andy, too."

"Who do you like better?"

"I don't know!" Amy fell back on the bed and stared at the ceiling in despair.

Tasha went into her matter-of-fact mode. "Well, you'd better decide. Because you can't have two boyfriends."

"Why not? Eric is here, Andy's three thousand miles away."

"It doesn't make any difference," Tasha said firmly. "You're only entitled to one boyfriend. That's the law."

Amy groaned. "Oh, bug off. You're giving me a headache."

Tasha dismissed that. "You never get headaches."

Once again Tasha was right. Amy's artificially constructed genes meant that she was always in perfect health. And she was more intelligent than the average twelve-year-old too. But for some reason, superior intelligence didn't make choosing boyfriends any easier.

Tasha looked at her watch. "It's almost time for *Crimesolvers*."

Amy climbed off the bed. "I want to check my e-mail first." She went to the computer on her desk and logged on to her Internet service provider. It always gave her a kick when she heard the mechanical voice announce, "Welcome! You've got mail!" She was even more pleased when she recognized the screen name of her correspondent.

"It's from Andy," she announced happily. When she left Paris, she and Andy had vowed to e-mail each other daily, and so far they'd kept their promise. She'd only been back two days, but even so . . .

She read the message silently to make sure there was nothing too personal in it. Then she read it aloud to Tasha. " 'The creeps in the Catacombs found out I was spying on them, so I can't go back there. Don't worry, I'm not in any danger, that gang is hopeless. Anyway, I'm almost through with school here, and my dad is meeting me in the south of France for a vacation. What's happening back in the good ol' USA? Miss you, Love, Andy.' "

She didn't have to explain the message to Tasha. Her friend already knew the whole story about the neo-Nazis Amy had encountered under the streets of Paris. They were a hateful group who were plotting to rid the world of all the people they considered undesirable.

But Tasha found something else in the letter more interesting. " 'Love, Andy'? *'Love'?*"

Amy grinned. "That doesn't mean anything. Everyone says 'love' at the end of a letter."

"I'm not so sure about that," Tasha declared. "Has Eric ever used the word 'love'?"

"Eric's never written me a letter," Amy countered. She pressed a key to save Andy's e-mail so she could read it again and answer it later. But what was she going to tell him? His life was now so much more exciting than hers. A description of her evening at the TV Diner couldn't compete with neo-Nazis in the Catacombs beneath Paris. Maybe there would be something interesting on *Crimesolvers* she could write him about.

The girls practically collided with Amy's mother, who was coming up the stairs as they raced down. "Where's the fire?" Nancy asked.

"Crimesolvers," the girls replied in unison, and Nancy groaned.

"How can you girls watch that show? It's so depressing!"

Amy thought her mother had to be the only person in the world who didn't like *Crimesolvers.* In the past month, it had become one of *the* most popular shows on TV. Any day now, there would be a menu item at the TV Diner named after it.

"I don't think *Crimesolvers* is depressing," Tasha commented as she took the remote and clicked. The local news was still on, and they had to sit through a report on an armed robbery downtown. "*That* is what's depressing, the regular news. You get the bad news, and that's all. At least on *Crimesolvers* they try to do something about all the terrible crimes."

The girls settled back comfortably on the sofa and waited for the news to end. There was only one more item, and fortunately it wasn't anything gruesome.

The anchorwoman was speaking. "And finally tonight, sources in the state department of education have announced that due to the unresolved budget situation, a temporary freeze will be imposed on the hiring of additional teachers in the Los Angeles County public schools."

Amy giggled.

"What's so funny?" Tasha demanded.

"I just got this picture in my head of teachers sleeping in the frozen foods section at the supermarket."

Tasha spoke reprovingly. "That's not what a hiring freeze is all about, Amy. This is serious. Right here in L.A., and all over the United States, we've got overcrowded classrooms, and a shortage of teachers, and—"

"I know, I know," Amy interrupted. "Shhh, it's *Crimesolvers.*"

The familiar theme music came on, and a somber voice declared, "Good evening, viewers, and welcome to another edition of *Crimesolvers.* I'm your host, Roger Graves." It was an appropriate name for the man, who faced the camera with a grave expression. "Tonight we invite you to help the authorities solve a crime on the highway," he continued. "This particular crime has nothing to do with a car chase or an accident. We're talking about the information superhighway and a crime that has been committed on the World Wide Web. Stay tuned for our first segment."

A commercial came on, and Amy turned to Tasha, wrinkling her nose. "I'll bet I know what this is. It's going to be a story about some dirty old guy who tries to flirt with little girls in chat rooms."

Tasha made a face. "Oh, gross, I hate that kind of story."

But that wasn't the issue of the evening. Roger Graves returned to the screen. "We all take the Internet for granted these days. We use it to communicate for both business and personal reasons. We use the Internet to seek information, to purchase everything from shoes to prescription medicines, to make connections. But every time we log on, every time we make a request or provide an address, we are giving someone information about ourselves. And information can be intercepted. Case in point—meet Martin L."

Martin L. turned out to be a man who used his computer a lot. Some thief had managed to hack into his line and had basically stolen his identity. Poor Martin L. not only lost money, he'd had his driver's license revoked and his credit destroyed, and he'd become a suspect in an international drug-selling scheme.

"You know, maybe you should be more careful about what you say in those e-mails to Andy," Tasha pointed out during the next commercial.

Amy laughed. "You think Eric's going to hack into my e-mail?"

"No. I'm thinking about the organization. Remember them?"

Amy stopped laughing. Tasha had a point.

Amy wasn't very likely to forget about the organization. Even though she hadn't encountered problems lately, the organization had a special, permanent place in the back of her mind.

Not long ago, Amy had learned the truth about her own birth. She'd learned that she had been created as part of Project Crescent, a top-secret government experiment in cloning. Her mother had been one of the project's scientists, who'd thought they were conducting research that would benefit humankind. Too late, they had discovered that the funding for the project had come from an organization dedicated to the creation of a master race. The organization wanted to use the exceptionally gifted beings who had been cloned in Project Crescent to achieve world domination.

The scientists weren't going to allow this to happen. They arranged for the twelve cloned infants to be distributed to orphanages and adoption agencies all over the world. Nancy Candler had taken Amy, Number Seven, home to raise as her own daughter. Then the scientists had deliberately set off an explosion, destroying the laboratory and all evidence of their research.

The organization was supposed to believe that the cloned babies had died in the explosion. But there was recent evidence that whoever they were, they hadn't bought the story, and even now, it was possible that all the Amys of the world (and all the Andys—a separate cloning experiment that had produced boys) were being watched. What the organization wanted from them, no one knew for sure—and Amy didn't think she ever wanted to find out.

So Amy knew she had to be discreet. She'd been warned about this by her mother, over and over again:

Don't show off, don't let people see how exceptional you are, don't talk about your origins. As for the crescent-shaped mark on her back—if asked, she would say it was a birthmark, nothing more. Which wasn't really a lie. All the clones in Project Crescent had been marked with a crescent moon.

But it had been a while since she had felt threatened by the organization. For all Amy knew, they could have given up on the clones by now.

The commercials were finally over, and the host returned to the screen. "Welcome back to *Crimesolvers*. It's been over two years since the body of a woman was discovered on a street in a small Indiana town. She was found behind the wheel of a car, shot in the back of the head. Evidence collected at the scene has led authorities to devise the following possible scenario."

This was what *Crimesolvers* did best—reenacting a crime. Amy felt like she was watching a real criminal act in progress, like she was actually seeing the victim and the bad guys, not actors. It was way unreal. The poor woman was shown picking up three hitchhikers, who killed her and took her money.

"If you know anything about this murder, if you can provide any clues, call *Crimesolvers* with your information. All calls will be kept confidential. . . ." As the host went on, the camera continued to show the actor-victim, her lifeless body bent over the steering wheel of her car.

The image brought back a memory, and Amy could feel the tears stinging in her eyes.

Tasha saw this. "Are you okay?"

Hastily Amy wiped her eyes. "Yeah, I was just thinking about something. Someone."

"Mr. Devon?"

Amy nodded.

Tasha knew all about Mr. Devon. He'd first appeared as an assistant principal at Parkside Middle School, where he'd helped Amy uncover her identity. Then he had disappeared. But every now and then, he had popped up when she needed him. Amy never knew his real identity. But somehow she knew he was always watching out for her.

Until the day she discovered him sprawled across the steering wheel of his car, like the woman in the crime she'd just seen reenacted. And like that woman, Mr. Devon was dead.

"They never found his killer, did they?" Tasha asked.

Amy shook her head.

In the final segment of the show, Roger Graves had the tiniest glimmer of a smile on his grim face.

"Now an update on a segment we showed you two weeks ago. Once again, our viewers came through with information that led to the solving of a particularly vicious crime." As he went on, Amy recalled the murder of a group of businessmen at a convention. They were ordinary people with no criminal background, and no one could understand why they'd been killed. It turned out that they were the victims of organized crime, a particularly violent gang called the Green Spiders, who had connections with various businesses and even with the government. The Spiders had developed a financial scam that they pulled off by removing certain leaders of the business community.

"The Green Spiders' leadership has been indicted by a grand jury, and their trial begins this week," Roger Graves reported. "Due to the notoriety of the gang and its connections, the trial will be conducted under tight security. We thank the anonymous viewer who called in the tip that led to their arrest. If you, or anyone you know, has information about a crime, or if you would like *Crimesolvers* to investigate an unsolved mystery, you can call this number twenty-four hours a day."

Amy looked at the number that flashed across the screen. She didn't have to write it down—her exceptional memory would keep it engraved in her mind for as long as she needed it. She got up, went to the phone, and began to dial.

"What are you doing?" Tasha asked.

"I just had an idea." She heard the phone at the other end ringing. It was answered by a recorded voice.

"Thank you for calling *Crimesolvers*. If you have information about a crime described on *Crimesolvers*, please press one. If you would like to report an unsolved mystery, please press two."

Amy pressed two. The voice told her to describe the unsolved mystery.

"A man named Mr. Devon was found dead in a car on a highway in Oregon." She went on to provide the date and time of the event. Then she hung up.

Tasha looked at her with approval. "Cool."

"It probably won't do any good," Amy said. "They must get tons of calls."

Still, it couldn't hurt. And it gave her something to write about in her next e-mail to Andy.

three 3

As Amy hurried to her homeroom Monday morning, she wondered if Ms. Weller would say anything about running into her at the TV Diner. Or would she act as if they hadn't even seen each other? Maybe Amy should say something to her first—but what? "Was that your boyfriend?" "What TV show did you eat?"

She probably shouldn't say anything at all. As her mother had told her, Ms. Weller was entitled to a private life. On the other hand, why should Amy pretend the encounter hadn't happened? If she'd run into one of her classmates, they would definitely say something about it that day at school. Why should teachers be different from classmates?

Because they were teachers. When Amy was little, she thought teachers lived in school. She remembered being seven years old and seeing her teacher in a drugstore, picking up a prescription. At the time, Amy had been shocked at the idea of a teacher being so human that she had to take medicine.

She knew better now, of course. Still, it was weird to think of teachers having nonteaching lives, as mothers, sisters, daughters, wives, people who went grocery shopping. Ms. Weller was her very favorite teacher, but that didn't make it any easier for Amy to picture her taking out the garbage. Or eating dinner with a boyfriend.

It was almost a relief to realize she wouldn't have to say anything. When she entered her homeroom, Ms. Weller wasn't at her desk. The pre-bell buzz emanating from the class was louder than usual as Amy slid into her seat. The girl who sat next to her stopped her scribbling and looked up.

"Hi, Amy. Were you sick?"

"No, I was in Paris, France, for a week," Amy replied. "My mother had to go to a conference there and I went with her."

"Oh." Claire Dudley didn't ask anything about Paris,

but at least she bestowed on Amy a fleeting smile and a comment: "Cool." She went back to what she'd been doing, her left arm curved around the sheet to hide what she was writing.

Amy remembered that Claire was a cheerleader, and she couldn't resist asking about the scandal. "I just heard what happened on the squad."

With obvious reluctance, Claire looked up again. "Yeah, it was pretty awful. Really embarrassing, you know, because it reflects on all the cheerleaders. It makes all of us look bad."

Amy tried to appear sympathetic. Claire was part of that stuck-up clique, but she wasn't as bad as some of them. At least she spoke to nonclique people, and once she had actually complimented Amy on her sweater.

"What are you guys doing about it?" Amy asked her.

"We've got to replace the girls who were let go as soon as possible," Claire replied. "All our routines are based on eight girls, and we can't do the cheers properly with only five. We're having a meeting this afternoon for tryouts." She cocked her head to one side and looked thoughtfully at Amy. "Are *you* going to try out?"

"No, but I have a friend who—" Amy's words were drowned out by the shrill bell that rang through the building. When the ringing ended, the desk at the front of the classroom remained empty, and the buzz in the classroom continued. Then the door opened and the principal walked in.

The buzz stopped abruptly. Dr. Noble had that effect on any room she entered. There was something about the dignified, authoritative woman that demanded instant respect. "Class, may I have your attention?"

She didn't have to ask. All eyes were already on her. Dr. Noble didn't visit classrooms just to say hi. She had a reason for being there. Somebody in that room could be in very big trouble.

Fortunately, that wasn't the case. "Your homeroom teacher, Ms. Weller, will not be here today. She's . . ." The principal hesitated for a second. "She has been called away for a while."

"Where to?" someone wanted to know, and at the same time another student asked, "Is she sick?"

Dr. Noble raised her hand in a gesture that stopped any more questions from coming. "That is not your concern," she said, pleasantly but firmly. "While Ms. Weller is away, a substitute teacher will be taking her place. Ms. Heartshorn is on her way here now."

What's the big deal? Amy wondered. Teachers were absent all the time, and it wasn't unusual to come into a class and find a substitute. Why was it necessary for Dr. Noble herself to come and tell them this?

"This will be Ms. Heartshorn's first experience as a substitute here at Parkside," Dr. Noble continued. "I trust that you will all behave yourselves and make her stay here a pleasant one."

Claire Dudley raised her hand. "How long will Ms. Weller be out? She's supposed to meet with the cheerleaders today. She's our faculty advisor."

Dr. Noble didn't exactly answer. "Ms. Heartshorn will be with you for a while," she said. "The office only learned about Ms. Weller's absence this morning, so we've just notified the substitute. She'll be here shortly. In the meantime, use the time wisely." With that, the principal left the room.

Immediately the buzz started up again, and if possible it was even louder now. Speculations and possible explanations flew across the room.

"Maybe Ms. Weller won the lottery!"

"Gee, she could be really sick."

Class clown Alan Greenfield put in his two cents. "Yeah, I bet we gave her a nervous breakdown."

"Nah, she's too cool for that."

"She's too cool to be a teacher. Maybe she got a better job."

"Yeah, like picking up garbage," Alan joked.

Claire was obviously more concerned about the cheerleaders than she was about any explanation for Ms.

Weller's absence, but even she had a suggestion. "She could have run off with her boyfriend."

Amy looked at her in surprise. "You know about him?"

"Who?"

"Her boyfriend."

Claire's eyes widened. "Ms. Weller has a boyfriend?"

"You just said—"

"I was simply guessing she might have a boyfriend," Claire said. "She's pretty good-looking for a teacher."

Amy suddenly wondered if Ms. Weller could be with Mr. Lasky right now on their honeymoon. It didn't seem possible. Ms. Weller would have told them if she was leaving to get married. Unless it was a spur-of-the-moment, spontaneous act. How romantic! Maybe right after Amy saw them at the TV Diner, they decided to elope. They could have run off to Paris!

In the midst of all the speculation, the intercom issued its three rings, which indicated that daily announcements were about to begin. In the noise of the classroom, Amy knew she was probably the only person capable of hearing the hollow voice.

"May I have your attention for the morning announcements? Today's Spanish club meeting has been canceled. All students interested in trying out for the cheerleading squad are invited to meet at three-thirty in the gym. Vision tests will be given this Friday, and permission slips are available in the office. The deadline to pay for the ninth-grade class trip . . ."

The classroom door swung open and a woman strode in.

The buzz died down as everyone turned to get a look at their substitute. Amy's first impression was—*gray*.

Everything about Ms. Heartshorn was gray. She had short, severely cut gray hair. She wore a shapeless gray suit. Even her skin had a grayish hue.

"Guess we don't have to worry about this one running off with a boyfriend," Claire whispered to Amy, and Amy suppressed a giggle.

But apparently she didn't suppress it well enough. Ms. Heartshorn was staring straight at her. "Do you have a joke you would like to share with the class?"

Amy swallowed. "No."

"What is your name?"

Amy could barely squeak out a response. "Amy Candler."

Ms. Heartshorn's small gray eyes bore into her, as if they were memorizing her face and her name. Then the teacher placed her briefcase on Ms. Weller's desk.

It was a big, heavy-looking case, very serious, with a combination lock in the lid. The class watched in silence as Ms. Heartshorn turned the combination dials

33

and opened it. Amy got the sense that the class was holding its collective breath as they waited to see what she was about to take out of the briefcase.

Amy got a brief glimpse of the paper the substitute extracted. It was a class seating chart. Ms. Heartshorn looked at the chart, then at the class. "Fourth row, third seat from the left. What is your name?"

"Linda Riviera," a trembling voice replied.

"You're in the wrong seat. Move two seats to your right." She paused. "To your *right*."

"Excuse me," Linda squeaked.

Ms. Heartshorn frowned. "You are a seventh-grader. You should know the difference between right and left." She moved around to the front of the desk.

"I am Ms. Heartshorn. I am replacing your teacher. Since this is the first time I have been a substitute at Parkside Middle School, I am not familiar with your routine. I do not know how your teacher conducted the homeroom period."

Here was a chance for Amy to make up for her earlier giggle. She raised her hand.

"Yes?"

"Well, usually Ms. Weller starts with—"

Ms. Heartshorn cut her off. "I don't recall asking you to tell me what Ms. Weller does."

Amy faltered. "I'm sorry, I—I thought you wanted—"

"Please," Ms. Heartshorn said coldly. "Make no attempt to anticipate what I want. As I was saying before I was so rudely interrupted, I do not know how your teacher conducted the homeroom period. I do not know, and I do not care. I will be establishing my own routine. I will begin by taking roll."

She lifted another paper out of the briefcase. "Adamson?"

"Here."

"Arnold?"

"Here."

"Bryant?"

"Here."

"Candler?"

"Here," Amy said. There was nothing different about the way the teacher said her name, and she didn't pause or make any comment. Without missing a beat, she went directly on to "Dudley." But Amy couldn't help thinking that Ms. Heartshorn's eyes had lingered on her a second longer than they had on anyone else. And she could have sworn she'd seen a flicker, the tiniest change in the teacher's face, at the moment when she said her name.

It was nothing, Amy assured herself. Ms. Heartshorn hadn't looked at her any differently than she was looking at everyone else. Amy was just feeling unnerved because the teacher had snapped at her, and she wasn't used to that. The change in Ms. Heartshorn's expression had probably just been her imagination.

Only, Tasha always told her she didn't have any imagination. It was true, Amy usually saw things as they really were.

In which case, Ms. Heartshorn's expression spoke louder than words. Amy had the uncomfortable, totally unfamiliar sensation of having been labeled a troublemaker.

fur

The buzz of homeroom was nothing compared to the noise in the Parkside Middle School cafeteria at lunchtime. But the deafening chaos didn't have anything to do with the fact that Tasha couldn't understand Amy's problem.

"I don't believe you," she said flatly.

"It's *true*," Amy insisted. "She *hates* me. Okay, maybe I'm exaggerating. But she doesn't like me."

"That's crazy," Tasha retorted. "Teachers always like you."

She was right, and Amy couldn't argue with her. Ever since kindergarten, Amy had always held a classroom position pretty close to teacher's pet. She was the smartest student, she was never absent, she was polite, and she never got into fights. What teacher *wouldn't* like her?

Ms. Heartshorn, apparently. "Tasha, you should have seen the way she looked at me."

Tasha still didn't appreciate her alarm. "So what? She's just a substitute."

"I know, but she might be around for a while."

"Why? What happened to Ms. Weller?"

"I don't know." The more Amy thought about the teacher's absence, the more concerned she felt. If Ms. Weller had known she was going to be away, she would have told the class. There must have been some kind of emergency.

"Is this teacher going to be substituting for Ms. Weller in English, too?" Tasha asked.

"I guess so." The prospect wasn't too appealing. And English was Amy's first class after lunch. Suddenly she lost her appetite. It was time for a change of subject.

"Did you hear that announcement this morning about the cheerleaders' meeting?" she asked Tasha.

Tasha nodded. "I'm going to it. Amy . . ."

Amy knew what was coming. "Yes, I'll go with you."

She couldn't blame Tasha for wanting a companion. *She* wouldn't want to face that stuck-up bunch alone either.

Throughout lunch, Amy kept her eye on the big clock at the back of the cafeteria. There was no way she would be late for English. She was determined not to get into any more trouble with Ms. Heartshorn.

She was in her seat five minutes before the bell rang to signify the start of the period. She was the first student in the room and the only student sitting there when Ms. Heartshorn walked in.

The teacher glanced at her but didn't smile or say a word. She went directly to the desk and placed the big briefcase on top. She didn't even acknowledge that Amy was there.

Amy wondered if she should say something and figured it couldn't hurt. So as Ms. Heartshorn manipulated the combination on the briefcase lock, she spoke, trying to sound both friendly and polite.

"How do you like Parkside so far, Ms. Heartshorn?"

Ms. Heartshorn opened the case. "I've been here for precisely four hours. It's too soon for me to make an evaluation." She looked up. "Why do you ask?"

"I was just curious," Amy said lamely.

Ms. Heartshorn began going through some papers. "You've heard the old saying about curiosity, Amy." She looked up again. "It killed the cat."

Amy felt like she'd been slapped. And now she was completely bewildered. *What* did this woman have against her?

At least it wasn't *just* her. No one else in the English class was treated any better. They all watched apprehensively as the substitute teacher glanced at their textbook. "You were supposed to have finished reading *The Adventures of Tom Sawyer* by today. I'm going to ask you some questions about it." She looked at the class roster. "Linda Riviera. Who wrote *The Adventures of Tom Sawyer*?"

"Mark Twain," Linda replied.

Ms. Heartshorn stared at her coldly. "Are you sure about that?"

Linda looked confused. "I think so."

Amy thought she knew what response the teacher wanted. She raised her hand, and Ms. Heartshorn nodded.

"Mark Twain was a pseudonym. The author's real name was Samuel Langhorne Clemens."

If she'd expected any praise for knowing this, she was in for a disappointment. Ms. Heartshorn looked back at the roster. "Jamison. In what year was *The Adventures of Tom Sawyer* published?"

Marc Jamison looked at her blankly. "In the nineteenth century."

"I didn't ask you in what century, I asked in what year."

"I don't know," Marc replied. "Ms. Weller didn't tell us we had to know the exact year."

"I didn't ask for an excuse, either," Ms. Heartshorn said. "Does anyone know the answer to this question?" She glanced at the roster and began calling names. "Duncan? Esterhaus? Mulroney?"

There was no response. Ms. Heartshorn gave the entire class a withering look. "This is pathetic. Not one person in this class can tell me in what year *The Adventures of Tom Sawyer* was published? Is this a remedial class? Are you all ignorant?"

Amy couldn't believe this. The nasty woman was calling them stupid! Amy wasn't going to stand for this. Fortunately, with her photographic memory, she could conjure up the page in the textbook that gave all the specific information about the book, and she mentally searched the page for the publication date. Without even raising her hand, she called out the answer.

"It was 1876."

Now the cold gray eyes were focused on her alone. "I do not recall giving you permission to speak."

Amy had to bite her tongue to keep from responding to that. The woman clearly did not encourage volunteers.

To the class in general, Ms. Heartshorn said, "Open your books and read the first chapter of *The Adventures of Huckleberry Finn*. You will be tested on it."

A murmur went through the class. Ms. Weller usually gave them an introduction to the book they were about to read, and they usually did the actual reading for homework, not in class. But no one brought this to the teacher's attention. They all seemed to have reached the same conclusion Amy had. Ms. Heartshorn was not interested in any information they could give her. Not to mention the fact that by now they were probably all as scared of the teacher as Amy was.

The first chapter of *Huckleberry Finn* was pretty short. With her ability to read at supersonic speed, Amy finished it in less than a minute. She kept the book open on her desk as she pondered the mystery of this substitute. But she was being too dramatic— this person wasn't a mystery, she was just a substitute teacher who didn't like to teach. Amy remembered having a substitute like that once before, a sour-faced woman who hated kids and didn't try to hide her feelings. Maybe that was why these people were substitutes and not regular teachers—they hated their jobs. That didn't make any sense, though. Why would they become teachers in the first place?

"Amy Candler." The voice cut through her thoughts like a knife. "Why aren't you reading?"

The tone of the teacher's voice was so irritating that this time Amy couldn't hold back. "Because I've already finished."

Ms. Heartshorn was unimpressed. In fact, Amy could tell that the teacher didn't believe her. "Oh, really? My, you must be very clever." The sarcasm dripped from her tongue. "Well, since you have so much time to spare, you may close your book and write a summary of the chapter."

An uncomfortably warm sensation came over Amy as she became aware of all her classmates' stares. She didn't think she'd ever been spoken to so rudely in her life.

"It was so embarrassing," she told Tasha later when they met at their side-by-side lockers. "Tasha, she's totally *mean*!"

"Maybe she's one of those teachers who acts mean

at first so she'll get respect," Tasha offered. "Remember how our elementary school teachers never smiled until November?"

"This isn't elementary school," Amy said. "And she's not getting respect, she's getting fear!"

"Well, maybe that's what she wants," Tasha said vaguely. Her thoughts were clearly elsewhere. Amy was more than willing to take her mind off Ms. Heartshorn and concentrate on Tasha's situation.

"Are you nervous about this meeting?" she asked her as they approached the entrance to the gym.

"A little," Tasha admitted. "I'm not exactly an athlete."

Amy could vouch for that. "But you can do cartwheels and splits, you can dance, and you've got lots of personality," she assured her friend. "Plus, you've got a big mouth. That's all you need to be a cheerleader."

She hoped she sounded more confident than she really felt. Having never been interested in cheerleading, she really didn't know what was required of them. At the basketball games, her eyes were usually fixed on Eric. As far as she could tell, all a cheerleader needed to do was jump up and down and yell a lot.

But according to Alison Ramirez, captain of the squad, a cheerleader needed more than energy and enthusiasm. "To be a cheerleader at Parkside Middle School is a great responsibility," she told the group solemnly. "You are responsible for communicating the spirit of the school. You are the symbol of Parkside, you represent Parkside. You *are* Parkside. Only very, very, very special girls can be cheerleaders."

Amy tried to figure out what was so special about the four other girls who stood alongside Alison on the gym floor. As far as she could see, the only interesting thing about them was the fact that they all had identical hairstyles, straight bobs that fell to just above their shoulders. She wondered if that was a requirement. If so, Tasha would have to get her curls straightened.

"We were planning to have the first round of tryouts today," Alison continued. "But our faculty advisor, Ms. Weller, isn't here, so they'll have to be postponed. If you're interested in trying out, please sign up and you'll be notified about the new date."

Tasha raised her hand. "What will we have to do at the tryouts?" she asked.

"We'll demonstrate a cheer, and then you'll have to do it," Alison replied.

Amy noticed a cheerleader whispering to another one. Months ago Amy had learned to read lips, and she tried not to use her skill too frequently. It was too much like eavesdropping. But sometimes when she was bored, like right now, she couldn't resist.

"I don't know why Tasha Morgan is worried about trying out," the girl was whispering. "It's not like she has a chance."

Amy's heart sank. It was so disgusting that these girls had probably already decided who they would pick. They shouldn't even bother having tryouts. Amy wondered whether she should tell Tasha what she'd just learned. She decided not to.

Ms. Weller had only just been appointed the cheerleaders' advisor, and Amy was sure she wouldn't let them get away with choosing their friends. She'd insist that the new cheerleaders be good at what they were supposed to do, not just have the right haircut or the right boyfriend. She hoped Ms. Weller would be back soon.

As Amy waited with Tasha in the sign-up line, Claire Dudley strolled over. "Amy, you changed your mind!"

"Huh?"

Claire smiled brightly. "You're going out for cheerleading."

"Oh, no, I'm not," Amy said quickly. "I'm just here with my friend Tasha. She wants to try out."

Claire's smile disappeared. "Oh." Her eyes swept over Tasha. Then she walked away.

She couldn't have been more obvious if she'd come right out and told Tasha, "Forget it." Amy glanced at her best friend worriedly. But Tasha didn't look like she was about to burst into tears. Her expression was only more determined.

"I'm going to show them," she told Amy on the way home. "I'm going to be so good at those tryouts, they'll *have* to choose me."

"Absolutely," Amy agreed. "As soon as we get home, I'll help you practice."

When they got back to their condo community, they didn't even stop for a snack. They went directly to Tasha's room so she could change into shorts and a T-shirt. But by the time they came back outside, Eric and a friend from the basketball team were on the driveway, shooting hoops. Tasha refused to practice on the lawn.

"I'm not going to jump around in front of *them*," she declared.

"If you make it onto the squad, you'll be jumping around in front of the whole school," Amy pointed out.

"Yeah, but then I'll be a real cheerleader, not just a wannabe," Tasha retorted. "So I won't care."

In a peculiar way, that made sense. Besides, Amy didn't really want to be out there with the boys either.

"Eric hasn't said one word to me since the restaurant," she told Tasha as they went upstairs to Amy's room.

Tasha wasn't deeply concerned. "Don't sweat it," she advised.

"That's easy enough for you to say," Amy countered. "He's your brother. You wouldn't care if he never spoke to you again."

"That's true," Tasha admitted. "But why would you want Eric if you can have Andy? Did you get an e-mail from him today?"

"I don't know," Amy said. "I'm going to check right now." She went to the computer, and while Tasha stuck a CD into Amy's player, Amy logged on.

She was very pleased to see that Andy continued to keep his promise. "He says he thinks it's cool that I called *Crimesolvers* about Mr. Devon. Oh, and he says to say hi to you and Eric."

"Hi back at him from me," Tasha said. "I can't speak for Eric."

Amy saved the message and turned. "Tasha, what are you doing?"

Tasha was staring at herself in Amy's mirror, pulling her curls back and studying her face. "What do you think I'd look like with straight hair?"

"You'd look like the other cheerleaders," Amy replied. "Is that what you want?"

Tasha let her curls drop and grinned. "No. I mean,

my whole point in trying to get on the squad is to show everyone you don't have to be one of *them* to be a good cheerleader."

"Exactly," Amy declared in approval. "That's a very cool attitude. Very mature."

"I know," Tasha said. "I just want to do something different to myself to celebrate. So I can *look* more mature."

"A makeover?" Amy suggested. "No, wait, I've got a better idea." She rummaged through a drawer and pulled out a package. "I got these at the airport duty-free shop in Paris when I wanted to get rid of my left-over French money."

Tasha examined the package. "Fake fingernails?"

"Two sets. They're supposed to look real, not like the Halloween kind. I've got polish and decals, too."

Tasha looked at her own stubby fingernails. "Okay. You can do mine and I'll do yours."

"You're on," Amy agreed. "Let's go downstairs."

On the dining room table, they set everything up—nails, glue, polish, decals, a bag of taco chips, and a bowl of salsa. They were still hard at work when Amy's mother came home.

"What are you girls up to?" she asked. Then she got a look at their hands. "Good grief."

Tasha waggled her elegant bloodred nails in the air. "I'm trying to decide between gold glitter and silver. What do you think, Ms. Candler?"

Nancy shook her head in resigned amusement. "I suppose it's better than a tattoo or a pierced nose."

"A tattoo on a cheerleader," Tasha said thoughtfully. "*That* would be different."

Nancy Candler sighed, then smiled. "I'm sure I can speak for your mother, Tasha, when I say don't even *think* about it. You're going to have a hard enough time explaining the nails." She looked at Amy's hands and let out an even deeper sigh. "Are you girls sure there aren't any rules at Parkside about fingernail length?"

"No rules," Amy assured her. "Unless Ms. Heartshorn decides to create a new set of laws for her classes. I wouldn't put it past her."

"Who's Ms. Heartshorn?" her mother asked.

"She was subbing for Ms. Weller today. Mom, she is so mean. Worse than mean, she's *evil*. She hates all the students. Especially me."

"Oh, Amy, don't exaggerate."

"I'm not exaggerating!" She told her mother about the events at school. "She was barking at everyone, and she *really* picked on me."

"Maybe she was nervous," Nancy suggested. "Did she ever substitute at Parkside before?"

"No."

"Then give the poor woman a break, Amy. It was her first day."

"I just hope it's also her last," Amy grumbled. She raised her eyes to the heavens. "Oh, *please*, let Ms. Weller be back in homeroom tomorrow morning."

f5ve

Amy's prayer wasn't answered. Ms. Weller was not in homeroom Tuesday morning. Or the next day, or the day after that. By Friday, Amy was a nervous wreck.

"Don't you *dare* tell me I'm being paranoid," she warned Tasha as they walked to school.

She knew Tasha wouldn't dare. Amy had been regaling her with horror stories about Ms. Heartshorn on the way to and from school every day that week. When she wasn't talking about the incidents, she was reliving them, over and over in her head. She felt like her brain had become a broken VCR that replayed the same scenes again and again.

Like the scene on Tuesday in homeroom. The usual morning announcements were coming over the intercom.

"We are pleased to announce that the Parkside debate team has reached the semifinals in the regional tournament. All students are encouraged to attend the debate to be held on Saturday at Highland Middle School and show their support for the Parkside team."

"Amy," Claire Dudley whispered. "Will you pass this to Karen?" She extended a folded piece of paper, and Amy took it.

The announcements continued. "Students are reminded that signed permissions for the vision screening on Friday are due in the office by Thursday."

Amy turned slightly toward Karen, who sat on her other side. Karen took the note.

"Amy Candler!"

Again that sharp voice was like the sound of a bullet. The class froze, and Amy could feel all eyes on her.

"You're not paying attention to the morning announcements," Ms. Heartshorn accused her.

Amy resisted the urge to say that no one ever paid much attention to the announcements. Ms. Heartshorn would not appreciate a smart-aleck answer. She just hoped her voice wouldn't tremble when she replied.

"I listened to the announcements, Ms. Heartshorn."

Ms. Heartshorn didn't believe her. "Oh, really? Then you won't mind repeating them to us, will you?"

Amy's fear began to dissolve, serious annoyance taking its place. Amy would show Ms. Heartshorn.

"We are pleased to announce that the Parkside debate team has reached the semifinals in the regional tournament. All students are encouraged to attend the debate to be held on Saturday at Highland Middle School and show their support for the Parkside team. Students are reminded that signed permissions for the vision screening on Friday are due in the office by Thursday," she said in one breath.

She had just repeated the announcements word for word. Would she now be accused of disrespecting the teacher? Ms. Heartshorn only looked at her, long and hard. Then she instructed the class to read quietly until the bell.

Amy's internal VCR then skipped forward to Wednesday, fourth period. Ms. Heartshorn was addressing the English class.

"Close your books. We are going to have a pop quiz."

Normally this kind of announcement was greeted with groans. But by now everyone was so scared of Ms. Heartshorn that the room remained silent as the teacher passed out the one-page quiz.

Amy scanned the page quickly. The questions dealt with the first chapter of *Huckleberry Finn*, and they were easy. Anyone who had actually read the chapter shouldn't have any problem answering the true-or-false questions.

"After his adventure with Tom Sawyer, Huck Finn received six thousand dollars. True/False." Amy circled "True."

"Huck ran away from the Widow Douglas. True/False." Again Amy circled "True."

"Huck went back to live with the Widow Douglas. True/False." "True."

"The Widow Douglas read Huck the story of Jonah from the Bible. True/False." This time Amy circled "False." The Bible story was about Moses.

All the questions were pretty much the same until she got toward the end. There she found fill-in-the-blank questions, and they were very specific.

"Tom asked Huck to join his band of _____."

"The sister of Widow Douglas tried to teach Huck what subject? _____."

"What kind of insect crawled into Huck's room? _____."

"On what part of Huck's body did the insect crawl? _____."

Ms. Heartshorn was a real nitpicker. Amy scrawled in the answers: *robbers; spelling; spider; shoulder.*

But the last question was really weird. "What is the last line in chapter one?" Amy wondered how many kids would be able to answer that one. She was pretty sure that normal people didn't have the photographic memory *she* had.

Carefully she wrote out the line. Then she put down her pencil.

Heartshorn must have been watching her. "Amy Candler, bring me your quiz." Amy rose and went to the desk at the front of the room. She handed the paper to the teacher and stood there silently as Ms. Heartshorn went over the answers, making little ticks with a red pencil next to each one as she read it.

As Amy expected, all her answers were correct. But Ms. Heartshorn didn't write "100" or "A+" at the top of the paper. Instead, she spoke accusingly to Amy.

"You cheated on this."

Amy gasped. "I did *not* cheat! I've never cheated on a test in my life!"

But her protests fell on deaf ears. "This last question . . . no one could write it as precisely as you did without copying it. You must have looked in your book while you were taking the test." And with that, she scrawled a big zero on the paper.

Amy was speechless.

For homework, they were assigned to read chapter two of *Huckleberry Finn* and compose a one-page summary. This time Amy tried to make the paper less than perfect. She purposely misspelled three words and made four grammatical errors.

Fast-forward to Thursday. The summaries were turned in. Ms. Heartshorn graded them and handed them back before the period was over. Amy received an F. Across the top of the paper the teacher had scrawled, "You can do better than this."

Amy began to be dimly aware that Tasha was snapping her fingers in Amy's face. "Earth to Amy. You want to beam back down to this planet?"

"Sorry," Amy said. "I was just thinking . . . I don't know who I hate more, Ms. Heartshorn or Huck Finn."

"At least you don't have to go to English today," Tasha pointed out.

"I don't?"

"You have English fourth period, right? That's when we're getting our eyes checked."

Practically all the students were taking advantage of the free screening, and Amy hadn't wanted to stand out by passing it up. So she'd brought in a permission slip, signed by her mother, even though both of them knew her vision was perfect. Personally, Amy would have been happy to have every one of her senses checked if it meant she could get out of a class with Heartshorn.

She still had to face the evil witch in homeroom, though. When Amy arrived, the teacher wasn't there yet, and there was an atmosphere of optimism in the class.

"Maybe Weller's back," Alan Greenfield said. "Or maybe we'll have a different substitute."

Another student walked in and heard him. "No, Heartshorn's here, I just saw her in the lobby."

Alan groaned, and another student, Layne, shrieked "Oh, no!" Amy thought that was an awfully dramatic response, but it turned out that Layne wasn't talking about the teacher.

"Nobody move! My contact lens fell out!"

Amy gazed at the floor around Layne. Her powerful vision came through, and she spotted the lens under the desk next to Layne's. "I see it," she declared, and bent down.

"Amy, you're amazing!" Layne squealed as Amy presented her with the tiny plastic lens.

"What's going on in here?" Ms. Heartshorn stood in the doorway.

"Amy found my contact lens," Layne said happily.

Ms. Heartshorn didn't seem to think this was a great accomplishment. In fact, she glared at Amy as if she'd done something very wrong. "Go back to your seat, Amy," she snapped. "And stay there!"

Amy did as she was told, but inside she was seething. Now she was feeling even more certain that she was being singled out for special abuse. What did this teacher have against her? And how much longer was she going to have to put up with this treatment?

Thank goodness for the vision screening. She was almost cheerful when she arrived in the cafeteria at noon, knowing she wouldn't have to go to English after lunch. Tasha didn't look very cheerful, though.

"You're not going to believe what I just found out," she told Amy glumly. "I've got a problem."

"What?"

"Cheerleaders can't wear glasses."

"Why not?"

"Because they can fall off when they're doing the routines. I *know* when I take that vision test, I'm going to find out I need glasses."

Amy shrugged. "So if you need glasses, you'll get contacts."

Tasha shuddered. "I can't stand the thought of putting those things in my eyes. Every time I see someone doing that, I feel positively sick."

She *did* have a problem. "What are you going to do?"

"I've come up with an idea," Tasha told her. "But I'm going to need your help. Have you ever had a vision screening?"

"No, what's it like?"

"You have to read letters off a chart. The letters get smaller and smaller, so if you don't have perfect eyesight, you can't see them all. That's how they know you need glasses."

Amy didn't understand how she could help. "I can't see for you, Tasha."

Tasha hesitated for a second. Then she plunged in. "Actually, you *can,* in a way. If you take the test first, you can memorize the letters, and after the test you can write them down for me. Then I'll learn them, and I'll be able to rattle them off whether or not I can see them."

"You think you'll be able to memorize the letters?"

"I know I don't have a memory like yours," Tasha said. "But a lot of people do it."

Amy considered Tasha's request. "It's sort of like cheating, isn't it?"

"Yeah, it is," Tasha admitted. "But it's for a good cause. Don't you want to see me become a cheerleader?"

"Of course I do," Amy replied. "And I've already been accused of cheating anyway, so I might as well do it for real."

They ate quickly and left the cafeteria early to scope out the vision test setup. Peering through the window in the classroom door, Amy thought Tasha's plan wouldn't be difficult to carry out. It was just the way Tasha had described. A screen had been set up, and a chair faced it. A man in a white coat was testing the projector that flashed the letters on the screen, while a couple of teachers stood by to assist.

Then Amy's heart sank. One of the teachers was Ms. Heartshorn. Was there no way on earth Amy could keep her distance from that woman? She was getting the awful feeling that the fates were throwing them together at every possible turn.

But she knew there wasn't anything spooky about Ms. Heartshorn's presence. It made sense that she'd be one of the teachers who had to help with the screening. Substitutes always got stuck with the jobs that the real teachers didn't want to do.

It didn't matter, anyway. The scheme was easy to pull off. As students began to line up for the test, Amy positioned herself near the front of the line. When it was her turn, she went into the room and gave her name. The other teacher checked her off. Ms. Heart-shorn was watching her, but she didn't say anything.

The man in the white coat pointed to the chair and gave her instructions. "Read the first line."

Amy read the letters. "L, Y, R, Q, O, P, B, C."

"Second line."

These were smaller. "M, X, A, G, D, F, J."

It went on like this, the letters becoming increasingly small. Still, Amy had no difficulty reading them. She had no problem committing them to memory, either.

The man in the white coat seemed impressed. "You have excellent vision," he pronounced. She left the room and met Tasha in the hall. "Okay, here goes," she said, and spoke softly so no one else could hear. "L, Y, R, Q, O, P—"

Tasha stopped her. "You're going to have to write them down if I'm going to memorize them."

"Okay," Amy said, and opened a notebook. Then she caught a glimpse of Ms. Heartshorn, looking out the window into the hall. From where the girls were standing, the teacher couldn't see what they were doing and wouldn't be able to hear them either, but Amy wasn't taking any chances. She closed the notebook. "Let's go to the library."

For a normal, average, ordinary human being, Tasha

did have an excellent memory. "I did it!" she told Amy triumphantly on the way home from school. "According to that man in the white coat, I have perfect vision!"

"Great!" Amy congratulated her. "Now, what are you going to tell your parents? You think they're going to believe that you have perfect vision? They're the ones who notice how you squint when you're watching TV."

"I'm going to tell them we didn't get the results right away. Then maybe they'll forget about it."

Amy doubted that. "They won't forget, Tasha. Especially when they see you squinting."

"So I'll have to remember not to squint. Hey, *Crimesolvers* is on tonight. Want to come over and watch it with us?"

"Okay," Amy said. It was always more fun to watch with a friend. Maybe Eric would watch the show with them. It would be a chance to start mending fences with him.

"Good," Tasha said. "Just remember to pinch me if you see me starting to squint."

It wasn't exactly easy for Amy that evening. She had to juggle watching *Crimesolvers* with keeping an eye on Tasha and trying to communicate nicely with Eric at the same time. It didn't help that the first case on the show dealt with a mail-order bride who was accused of killing her husband.

64

"That figures," Eric said. "She uses the guy as a ticket to get out of her crummy country and come to America. Then, as soon as she gets here, she knocks him off. Typical."

"Typical of what, Eric?" Mrs. Morgan wanted to know.

"Women," Eric declared. "They always betray men." After a second he added, "No offense intended, Mom." Amy knew exactly who the offense was intended for. She glanced at Tasha, whose forehead was puckered—the first sign that she was about to start squinting. Amy pinched her, and Tasha's expression cleared.

At least the second case didn't have anything to do with love, marriage, or betrayal. Unfortunately, it was about the disappearance of an American tourist in Paris. Amy didn't have to look at Eric to know that every time the city was mentioned, his scowl deepened. Which reminded her to pinch Tasha again before her mother noticed her squint.

But after a commercial break, the next case made her forget all about Tasha's squint and Eric's lousy mood.

"In a black sedan, in the parking lot of a convenience store just off Highway 61 in southern Oregon, a man by the name of Devon was discovered sitting in the driver's seat."

Amy drew in her breath sharply, and she could hear Eric do the same. Tasha edged closer to the TV screen.

"Devon was dead," Roger Graves continued. "He had not been robbed, and detectives have been unable to determine why he died. An autopsy did reveal that he'd been kicked in the solar plexus by someone who knew martial arts. If you or anyone else has any information about this case, please call *Crimesolvers*."

"I'm going to make some popcorn," Mrs. Morgan announced, and left the room. As soon as she was out of earshot, Amy turned to Tasha excitedly. "I can't believe it! They actually put it on TV!"

"How did they find out about Mr. Devon?" Eric asked.

"Amy called the TV show," Tasha told him.

Eric was impressed. "Really?"

Amy nodded. "It's always bothered me, not knowing who killed him, or why. Or even how!"

"I remember," Eric said. "You told us you didn't see any blood."

"Maybe they'll get a real clue," Tasha said. "This show has a huge audience."

"And then next week they'll do one of those reenactment things," Eric added.

Now Amy was doubly excited. Not only was there a possibility of Mr. Devon's murder being investigated, but also Eric was actually speaking to her again!

Mrs. Morgan returned with the popcorn, so they

had to stop talking about Mr. Devon. Roger Graves was now presenting the updates on previously reported crimes.

"A viewer called in with some significant information that is leading detectives closer to a possible resolution in the case of Martin L., the man whose identity was stolen by computer hackers. There is an indication that the crime was set in motion by a notorious gang of Canadian drug runners who have developed computer expertise. Police inform us that an arrest is imminent.

"Also, in the trial of the Green Spiders, the gang accused of murdering businessmen at a Los Angeles convention, there are reports that potential witnesses have received anonymous death threats. There is even a report that threats of retaliation have been made against the sequestered jury. Authorities are investigating.

"That's all for tonight. Thank you for watching *Crimesolvers*. If you or anyone you know . . ." He went on to give the usual instructions about calling the program. As soon as the show was over, Amy got up.

"Are you leaving?" Tasha asked.

Amy nodded. "I have to e-mail . . ." She remembered that Eric was in the room. ". . . you know," she finished lamely. "People." She said her goodbyes to Mrs. Morgan and Tasha.

"See you tomorrow," Tasha said.

To Amy's joy, Eric echoed that. "See you tomorrow," he said.

She flashed him a big smile, and her heart was lighter as she ran across the lawn to her own door. Eric was speaking to her normally again, and that was a good start to repairing their relationship.

As long as he didn't find out who she was racing home to write to.

"How do I look?" Tasha asked nervously.

Amy was with her in the gym's locker room Monday afternoon. She knew exactly what Tasha wanted to hear, and she said it.

"You look like a cheerleader. Not like all the other cheerleaders, of course. Like a distinctive, unique cheerleader." The official tryouts were being held that afternoon. Amy had agreed to go along with Tasha to lend moral support.

Tasha grinned. "You know, Amy, I really think I have a chance."

"I hope so," Amy said. "Especially considering how much time we spent practicing this weekend."

The tryouts weren't going to be anywhere near as competitive as they'd thought—only six other girls were trying out, and there were three vacancies on the squad. Amy was feeling more and more optimistic for her friend. She just hoped the new faculty advisor wouldn't let the current cheerleaders base their selections on cliques.

Raising her voice so the other girls in the locker room could hear her, Amy asked a general question: "Does anyone know who the advisor is?"

Her question was answered with shrugs and headshaking.

"What happened to Ms. Weller, anyway?" one of the girls asked.

"I heard she ran off with her boyfriend," someone said.

Another prospective cheerleader had a different answer. "No, that's not true, she won the lottery and she's living on the beach in Malibu."

Amy shook her head. "Those are just rumors."

"Then where is she?"

Amy had no answer.

"I wish you would try out too," Tasha wheedled.

"You'd be better than anyone. They wouldn't dare not choose you."

Tasha was probably right. With her skills, Amy could blow the rest of them away. "But my mother would kill me," she reminded Tasha. "This is exactly what I'm not supposed to do, draw attention to myself. Besides, I have absolutely no interest in cheerleading. Come on, let's go."

Amy tried not to consider the possibility that Ms. Heartshorn would turn out to be the new cheerleading advisor. But in all likelihood, she would. After all, Ms. Weller had been the advisor, and Ms. Heartshorn—even though she didn't seem like the kind of teacher who would enjoy coaching cheerleaders—*was* Ms. Weller's substitute. Amy steeled herself for facing her enemy.

It was a good thing she did. At least that way she was able to refrain from shrieking when she saw Ms. Heartshorn sitting with the cheerleaders on the bleachers in the gym.

"Oh no," Tasha breathed. *"Her."*

Amy hastened to reassure her friend. "It's me she hates—she doesn't even know you."

"But she's seen me with you," Tasha moaned. "She knows I'm your friend."

"Don't worry about it," Amy ordered her. "Just do

your best." She avoided making any eye contact with the teacher and took a seat on the bleachers as far as possible from the cheerleaders.

Down on the gym floor, Alison Ramirez called the cheerleading hopefuls together. "Claire and I are going to show you some moves," she told the girls. "Then you're going to do them."

As soon as they got into the first cheer, Amy began to worry. She'd never really paid much attention to what cheerleaders actually did. Now, for the first time, she realized that the moves were a lot more complicated than she had thought. She wasn't sure Tasha would be able to keep up.

But Tasha made a real effort. Her kicks and her jumps weren't as high as some of the other girls', and her tumbling wasn't as fast, but she was clearly putting her heart and soul into it. Amy thought she looked good. She strained to hear what the cheerleaders—and Ms. Heartshorn—were saying about the group.

"Okay, we'll take Lisa and Marie," one of them was saying. "But we still need a third."

Amy knew who Lisa and Marie were. Both were in the clique.

"Camilla Burns is okay," another cheerleader said. "She goes with Alan Parks, and he's captain of the football team."

"Which one is she?"

"Third from the left."

Amy focused on the girl they were talking about. She couldn't believe it—Camilla was no better than Tasha. And just because she was going with a football player, they were going to choose her to be a cheerleader!

Heartshorn wasn't agreeing, but she wasn't objecting, either. In fact, she wasn't saying a word. She was just going to let them continue making the cheerleading squad their own little private club.

Fury rose up within Amy. "Those snotty little rats," she said to herself, fuming. She waited for a break in the cheerleading routine being performed on the gym floor. Then she jumped up.

"Excuse me! I was just wondering if *I* could try out?"

Alison frowned. "You can't. You're not signed up."

Claire at least was kinder. "I wish you'd told us earlier that you wanted to try out, Amy. First we need a signed permission from a parent and a doctor's note saying you're healthy."

Then an unpleasantly familiar voice spoke from the bleachers. "I think you can make an exception this time. I'll give her permission to try out."

Amy was taken aback. What was this all about? Was Heartshorn trying to make up for all her nastiness?

Tasha looked surprised too, but she was pleased. Amy took a place in the line of prospective cheerleaders and watched as Alison and Claire demonstrated a routine. An image of her mother's disapproving face flashed across Amy's mind. Amy was supposed to be very careful not to show off her skills, but she was too mad to care. Let these snobs see what someone in superior physical condition could do with their stupid cheerleading routines. After she was chosen, she'd just tell them to stuff it.

"Okay, get ready," Alison shrieked. "One, two, three! Let's go, Parkside! Go, go, go!"

Amy went to work. While the other candidates moved hesitantly, trying to follow Alison and Claire, Amy already had the routine firmly imprinted on her mind. She moved with assurance and confidence. Her kicks were higher, her leaps sent her head and shoulders above the others. She twirled and twisted with grace and perfect rhythm, and her tumbling was fast and sure. She considered throwing in a little something extra—maybe a double spin in the air—but decided that would be too much. Still, she couldn't resist allowing herself one airborne spin, something she knew the average cheerleader—or the average human being—couldn't do.

She was rewarded by the expressions she saw on

the faces of the cheerleaders sitting in the bleachers. No one said anything. But she could tell how impressed they were. Every one of them was staring at her, and they were clearly overwhelmed. Ms. Heartshorn, however, wasn't reacting at all. She was just looking at Amy in that same cold, expressionless way.

"That will be all," Alison announced. "The names of the new cheerleaders will be posted on the lobby bulletin board tomorrow morning."

Back in the locker room, Amy was congratulated by two of the candidates, and Lisa and Marie, the two clique girls, were actually looking at her with nervous envy.

"You've got it," Tasha said as they left the school. "They have to choose you."

"It won't hurt your chances," Amy assured her. "Tomorrow I'm telling them that I don't want to be on the squad."

"Don't do that on my account." Tasha sighed. "I did okay, but it's not like I was better than anyone else. They'll choose Lisa and Marie and you, and then when you say no they'll pick another girl who has the right kind of hair."

"You don't really care, do you?" Amy asked. "It's not going to break your heart if you can't be a cheerleader?"

"No," Tasha said, but there was a slight wistfulness

in her voice that Amy didn't miss. Her friend needed some cheering up.

"Let's go to Bailey's," she suggested, and Tasha readily agreed.

Bailey's was a new ice cream place that had recently opened near Parkside. It was outrageously expensive; ice cream cost twice what it would at a Baskin-Robbins, and the prices discouraged middle school students from turning it into a hangout. But Amy had just received her allowance that morning, and Tasha needed a treat.

The place even looked expensive, with dim lighting, soft music, and fancy little wrought-iron tables and chairs. There were more adults in the place than children, and the soft hum of conversation gave it a café atmosphere.

The girls took a table and studied the menu. It offered sophisticated flavors, like Italian mocha cappuccino swirl and bittersweet almond fudge ripple. Amy settled on French vanilla with chocolate truffles and fresh mint leaves, while Tasha chose the frosted apricot meringue soufflé. They had just placed their orders when Amy noticed someone walking into the place.

"That man looks familiar," she murmured.

As if he'd heard her, the man looked in her direction. At that second, Amy realized where she knew him from. "It's Ms. Weller's boyfriend!" she whispered excitedly to Tasha. She waved to him. "Mr. Lasky!"

For a moment he looked blank. Then his eyes lit up in recognition, and he came over to the table.

"I know you!" he said. "You're one of Bonnie's students!"

"Bonnie?" It dawned on her that that must be Ms. Weller's first name. "Right, I met you at the TV Diner."

Mr. Lasky nodded. "I remember that," he said. "But I'm sorry, I don't recall your name."

"Amy Candler. And this is my friend Tasha Morgan."

Mr. Lasky and Tasha exchanged "pleased to meet you"s, and then Amy asked about Ms. Weller. "Is she sick or something? She's been out of school for a week. I hope she's okay."

"I hope so too," he said with a wan smile.

"You don't know what's happened?" Amy asked in surprise.

"I don't know anything!" the man exclaimed. "I've been calling, and I went by her place twice. She's not there."

Tasha drew her breath in sharply. "Are you sure? Maybe she's lying unconscious in her apartment!"

"I thought of that," Mr. Lasky said. "Bonnie's next-door neighbor has a spare key to her apartment. We went inside, and it was empty."

"Was there any sign of a struggle?" Tasha asked.

He shook his head. "No, everything looked normal."

"Were any clothes missing?" Amy wanted to know.

"I didn't check her closets." He looked like he was about to blush. "I don't know if I would have been able to tell if anything was missing. We've only been going out for a few weeks."

"Oh, I thought you two were more, you know, like a couple," Amy said.

He smiled, but it wasn't a happy smile. "I wish. I'm crazy about her. And I was thinking that she was beginning to feel the same way about me. I tell you, Amy, Tasha, I'm worried sick. I've called people we both know, even hospitals . . ." His voice trailed off.

"Did you call the police and report her as a missing person?" Amy asked.

"No. I figured if there was any mystery about her disappearance, your school would notify the police."

Amy had no idea if the school had alerted the police. "I'll see what I can find out," she told Mr. Lasky.

"That would be great," he said warmly. "I'll give you my number." He took a napkin and scrawled "Dan Lasky" and a phone number on it. "Would you call me if you learn anything?"

"Absolutely," Amy promised. She tore the napkin in half and wrote her name and number on the other piece. "Maybe you could call me if you find out anything first, okay?"

"Sure thing," he said. "I hope we'll be talking soon, and that we'll be sharing some good news." With a wave, he left the ice cream parlor.

"Wow, he really must be worried," Tasha commented. "He forgot to get any ice cream."

Amy sighed. "Well, that takes care of one of the rumors. Ms. Weller didn't run off with her boyfriend." And Amy wasn't holding out much hope that Ms. Weller had won the lottery, either.

seven 7

When they arrived at school the next morning, Tasha ran on ahead of Amy into the lobby.

"They didn't pick you, did they?" she asked when she caught up to Tasha by the bulletin board. Her friend looked dismayed.

"No. And they didn't pick you, either."

"You're kidding!" But there it was in black and white.

The following students have been selected to join the Parkside Middle School Cheerleading Squad: Lisa Aronson, Camilla Burns, Marie Lazaro.

"That's disgusting," Amy declared. "I was better

than any of them!" Hastily she added, "And you were just as good."

"Well, it's pretty much what I expected," Tasha said. "They only pick their friends, even when someone else is clearly better. I can't believe the faculty advisor let them get away with that. Even Heartless Heartshorn had to see how wrong this was."

Amy shrugged. "Nobody listens to faculty advisors." But even so, she had to agree with Tasha. Heartshorn didn't like her, that was clear, but teachers could usually be counted on to be fair.

Not in this situation, though. Amy learned that when she walked into her homeroom. Ms. Heartshorn wasn't there yet, and Claire Dudley was eager to speak to her.

"Amy, I am so furious!" she said. "You would have been a fabulous cheerleader. You can really move!"

Claire really seemed sorry, so Amy tried to believe that at least one cheerleader had tried to be fair. "I guess the others on the squad didn't feel the same way you did," she said.

To her surprise, Claire shook her head violently. "But they did! We all wanted you to be on the squad. Well, most of us did," she amended. "The majority voted for you."

"Then why didn't you choose me?"

"Ms. Heartshorn wouldn't let us."

"*What?*"

"It was so weird," Claire went on. "She said she didn't like the way you moved. She told us you'd make the rest of us look bad. I guess that makes sense. . . ."

Amy didn't think so. As far as she could see, Ms. Heartshorn was just taking one more step toward making Amy's life miserable. This was too much! Amy wasn't going to put up with it anymore.

As soon as Ms. Heartshorn walked into the room, Amy went to the teacher's desk and spoke, even before the teacher could put her big briefcase down. The cold gray eyes gave Amy the creeps, but she fought off the shivers.

"Ms. Heartshorn, I need to talk to you."

"Go to the principal's office," the teacher said.

Amy stared at her in disbelief. Was the witch punishing her for *speaking*?

"Dr. Noble wants to see you."

Now Amy really began to worry. No one was called to Dr. Noble's office unless they were in trouble. Or unless something had happened at home . . .

Her heart in her mouth, Amy raced down the hall and through the lobby to the administrative offices.

The bell hadn't rung yet, so teachers were still picking up mail and memos. That was why she didn't see Tasha right away.

It wasn't until she made it to the secretary's desk that she realized Tasha was there. She too looked really scared. "What's going on?" she asked Amy.

"I don't know," Amy replied.

But they both found out soon enough. Dr. Noble's door opened, and the intimidating principal beckoned to them both to come into her private office. She did not look happy.

She got right to the point. "A strange accusation has been made against the two of you. I'm going to ask a question, and I hope you will answer me honestly. Did you two cheat on your vision screening?"

Both Amy and Tasha stared at her dumbly for a minute. Then, simultaneously, they nodded.

"I don't understand," Dr. Noble said. "Why did you feel the need to cheat? Are you so afraid of wearing glasses?"

Tasha hung her head and confessed. "I wanted to try out for cheerleading, and I heard that cheerleaders aren't allowed to wear glasses."

Dr. Noble frowned. "I've never heard of that rule."

"Because they might fall off while you're jumping around," Tasha explained.

"That's ridiculous," Dr. Noble stated. "You would just need one of those bands that hold the glasses on your head. Many athletes wear glasses."

Amy looked at Tasha's face and saw the same shame she herself was feeling. Why hadn't they thought of that?

"But even if that was true," Dr. Noble continued, "it doesn't justify cheating on the vision test."

"I'm sorry," Tasha said humbly.

"I'm sorry too," Amy echoed.

"There's something else I don't understand," the principal said. "*How* did you cheat?"

"I went first and memorized the chart," Amy said. "Then I wrote down the letters and Tasha memorized them."

"Well, I advise you to put those excellent memories to better use," Dr. Noble said. "As punishment, you will both have detention after school for the next three days. And you'll both take the eye test again. The chart has been set up in the clinic. You can go there now."

The girls rose and started toward the door. But before she walked out, Amy looked back at the principal. "Dr. Noble . . . how did you find out that we cheated?"

"You were observed by a teacher," the principal replied. "Now, hurry up and go take your eye test so you won't miss the entire homeroom period."

As soon as they'd shut the door behind them, Amy looked at Tasha, and in unison they said, "Ms. Heartshorn."

"It had to be her," Amy said as they walked down the hall to the clinic. "She was there and looked out at us in the hallway at one point."

"But how could she tell we were cheating?" Tasha asked in bewilderment. "She might have seen us talking, but she couldn't hear what we were saying!"

Amy didn't have any answers. "This is so embarrassing," she moaned. "I wanted to ask Dr. Noble if she knew anything about Ms. Weller. But she'll never tell me anything now. She thinks I'm a criminal."

Apparently the nurse had been informed of their criminal act. "You, wait out in the hall," she ordered Amy sternly as she ushered Tasha inside the clinic.

Waiting, Amy fumed. The substitute was out to get her, there was absolutely no doubt in her head now. But *why*? She was more determined than ever to find out. And she vowed she would not leave school that day till she got some answers.

Tasha emerged from the clinic with a resigned expression on her face. "I need glasses," she announced. "Big surprise."

"We'll go to the mall this weekend and pick out cool

frames," Amy said. "See you at lunch." She went into the clinic. The nurse ushered her into a back room where a man in a white coat was waiting.

"Don't think you're going to pull any pranks this time," the nurse warned her. "You're not getting the same letters your friend had."

Amy slumped into the seat and looked straight ahead. "Read the first line," the man told her.

She did. "Y, O, U, A, R, E, I."

"Second line."

"N, S, E, R, I, O."

"Third line."

"U, S, T, R, O."

"Last line."

"U, B, L, E."

The nurse stuck her head in. "How did she do?"

"Perfect," the man replied.

"Are you sure?" the nurse asked suspiciously. "You can't trust these kids."

Amy wished for a hole to open up in the ground so she could fall through and disappear. She was utterly mortified.

The nurse sent her back to homeroom, and as she went down the hall, Amy tried to shake off the humiliation and concentrate on the conversation she planned to have with Ms. Heartshorn. But there was something hovering in the back of her mind. Something to do with that vision test . . .

The letters she'd just read off reverberated in her head. "Y, O, U, A, R, E, I, N, S, E, R, I, O, U, S, T, R, O, U, B, L, E." Then she realized she was spelling out a sentence. "You are in serious trouble."

The impact of the sudden realization stopped her in her tracks. She knew her mind wasn't playing any tricks on her. She wasn't inventing this. That was what the letters spelled.

Her head was spinning. What did it mean? Was someone sending her a message? But who? And why? Was someone trying to scare her? The man in the white coat? The nurse?

The bell rang. Students poured out of their homerooms to go to first-period classes. Amy just stood still, trying desperately to get a grip on herself. She considered running back to the office and getting permission to call her mother. She knew Nancy would stop whatever she was doing, jump in the car, and come to get her. She'd make sure Amy was safe.

But that wouldn't answer any questions. And Amy wanted answers.

She'd left her books in homeroom, so she had to go

back there to retrieve them. Ms. Heartshorn was still at the desk in the empty room, writing something on a pad. The teacher barely glanced at Amy when she walked in.

Feelings churned inside Amy. Anger, frustration . . . and now, real fear. She went to the teacher's desk.

"Ms. Heartshorn . . ."

"Yes?" The teacher stopped writing and looked up.

"Why do you hate me?" Amy blurted out.

Ms. Heartshorn didn't appear to be startled by the question. The gray eyes were calm and steady.

"I don't hate you."

"Then what's going on?" Amy demanded. "Why are you picking on me like this?"

The teacher tapped her pen on the desk. She looked like she was considering the question very carefully. But at that moment a boy appeared at the door.

"Ms. Heartshorn? There's a telephone call for you in the office."

"Thank you," Ms. Heartshorn said. She got up and started toward the door.

"Ms. Heartshorn!" Amy cried out in protest.

The teacher looked back at her. "You'd better get to your class, Amy, or you'll be late." She left the room.

Amy's fists were clenched so tight she could feel

her fingernails cutting into the palms of her hands. *Something* was going on. But clearly, she wasn't going to get any information easily.

Well, maybe she could find out something on her own. The substitute's briefcase was still sitting on the desk. Amy looked at the combination dials.

Her mind went back to the time she saw Ms. Heartshorn open the briefcase. Concentrating, she visualized the way the teacher had moved the dials. It took some real effort, but finally the precise movements were clear in her head.

She adjusted the three dials to three different numbers. Then she pressed the latch, and the briefcase made a little popping sound. She opened it.

The contents didn't look terribly interesting. There was a weekly newsmagazine lying on top. Under that were some papers with the school letterhead on them. There was a memo about a faculty meeting, and some announcements about health benefits. She saw class rosters and the teaching editions of several textbooks.

She dug in deeper. There had to be something personal in here, a letter maybe, something that would give her a clue as to what this woman was all about. She glanced at the door. Ms. Heartshorn could be back any minute. She didn't have much time.

Feeling around the bottom of the pile, her fingers touched something that was different . . . smaller than the papers, thicker, slick and glossy. A photograph, maybe? She tugged at the corner of it and pulled it out.

It *was* a photograph. A photograph she'd seen before.

It was her own picture, taken for the school yearbook.

e8ight

"**W**hat are you doing?"

Amy looked up at the figure standing in the doorway. Ms. Heartshorn's gray eyes were cold, but Amy's own brown eyes directed a frigid stare right back at her. Any fear she'd been feeling had now drowned in a flood of rage.

"What are *you* doing?" she demanded. "With *this*?" She indicated the photo.

For a split second, the teacher almost seemed to be at a loss for words. She recovered quickly, though. "I was given pictures of the students—"

Amy stopped her. "There are no other photographs

of students in your briefcase." Actually, she couldn't be positive about this. She hadn't had time to search thoroughly, but it was just too much of a coincidence that the one and only photo she would pull out would be of herself.

"I want the truth," Amy said, impressed with how forceful and determined she sounded. Her statement was punctuated by the ring of the bell.

"You're late for first period," Ms. Heartshorn said.

"It doesn't matter," Amy replied. "I already have detention."

Fortunately, no class was scheduled for this room. It was utterly silent. Even so, Ms. Heartshorn turned and shut the door. Then she pulled down the shade to cover the door's window.

Amy tensed up. Teachers very rarely pulled down that shade. Every part of her mind and her body went on alert. Ms. Heartshorn wasn't too much taller or bigger than she was . . . Amy could take her on.

But Ms. Heartshorn didn't rush to attack, nor did she display a weapon. She took a seat in the front row of the classroom and motioned for Amy to take the seat alongside her. "I want to talk to you."

Remaining on alert, Amy slipped into the seat. "I'm listening."

Ms. Heartshorn made a "tsk, tsk," sound, as if this

was all a big nuisance. "It's really much better for you if I remain incognito. That means unidentified. In disguise."

"I *know* what incognito means," Amy said. "I happen to have a very large vocabulary for my age."

"Yes," Ms. Heartshorn said. "I'm aware of that. Which precisely relates to the reason I am here."

"My vocabulary?"

"Your uninhibited, unrestrained use of vocabulary."

Amy looked at her without any comprehension at all. Ms. Heartshorn read that in her expression.

"You don't know what I'm talking about, do you?"

Amy hated to admit it, but clearly there was no other way she was going to get anything out of this woman. "Not a clue," she said.

Ms. Heartshorn rapped her nails on the desk. "Let me see, how can I explain this so you'll understand?"

"It shouldn't be that difficult," Amy replied. "I'm very intelligent for my age."

Ms. Heartshorn frowned. "There you go again!"

"Huh?"

"Letting the world know that you're a superior form of being."

Amy held her breath. "I don't know what you're talking about."

Now Ms. Heartshorn became testy. "I know all

about you, Amy. You are a genetically designed clone from Project Crescent. Where did you get that pendant you're wearing? From Dr. Jaleski?"

"You—you knew Dr. Jaleski?"

"I know *of* him. We never met personally. I do know that you made contact with him. And that he died shortly after."

"That wasn't my fault," Amy declared. She could feel the tears coming to her eyes as she remembered the director of Project Crescent, the man who had been like a father to her.

Ms. Heartshorn looked at her distastefully. "For someone who should have superior control of her emotions, you cry very easily."

"I'm not crying. It's—it's allergies."

"You don't have allergies," the teacher said. "You have perfect health."

Amy glared at her. "How do you know so much about me?"

"Because that's why I'm here. To save you."

"I'm not in any danger!" Amy objected. "No one's been bothering me."

"To save you from yourself."

"Excuse me?"

"You need someone to watch over you, young lady.

Someone to keep you in line. You've become careless and indiscreet. Too many people other than your mother know about your origins."

"Only Tasha and Eric," Amy said.

"That's two too many. And you haven't been properly cautious. You demonstrate your unusual memory, which is a dead giveaway. You display above-average athletic skills. You write freely on the Internet, which is easily intercepted. This is how we became aware of your indiscretions. Your e-mails to a boy currently living in Paris."

"Andy," Amy said. "He's like me."

"I know, I know," Ms. Heartshorn said impatiently. "But it is simply not appropriate for you to use an accessible communication system to discuss your situation. This has to be kept a secret. Your mother must have told you that."

Amy's head was spinning from the verbal assault. "Who *are* you?" she asked urgently. "Where do you come from?"

"I am here in the same capacity as Mr. Devon."

Amy became very still. "Oh."

She'd never known much about Mr. Devon, why he was watching her, where he had come from. Whenever she'd asked him, he'd refused to tell her anything.

And he was a nicer person than Ms. Heartshorn. It wouldn't be worth the effort to try to get any information from her.

"So . . . you're like my . . . my guide? My advisor? And you were going to keep that a secret?"

"It was safer for you if I simply appeared as a strict teacher."

"Strict? Ha! That's putting it mildly."

"Don't be rude," Ms. Heartshorn scolded. "I'm still your teacher. And you will do what I tell you to do."

Amy bristled. "I can take care of myself. I don't have to take orders from you."

"Yes, you do. Ask your mother."

Amy's mouth fell open. "My mother knows about you?"

"As for taking care of yourself, you're not doing a very good job. You're taking tests too quickly and making perfect scores. That little stunt with the eye exam was very bad. No one is supposed to be able to see all those letters. As for your performance with the cheerleading tryouts . . ." She shook her head wearily.

"But you allowed me to try out!" Amy protested.

"I wanted to see how far you would go, if you had any self-control at all."

"Well, I *do*. I could have done those cartwheels twice as fast."

"Yes, I know. But the cartwheels you did were faster than anyone else's. Is there anything more you'd like to do to call attention to yourself? I'm surprised you didn't jump off the top of the Eiffel Tower just to show the Parisians that you could land on your feet."

Wow! Ms. Heartshorn could be sarcastic. But at least this explained why the teacher had been picking on her.

There was still another question that hadn't been answered. "What happened to Ms. Weller?"

"You don't need to know anything about Ms. Weller."

"Can you tell me if she's okay? Everyone's wondering about her."

"Again, you don't need to worry about Ms. Weller. Please discourage any rumors you hear."

"It would be a lot easier for me to kill the rumors if I could tell people something else," Amy pointed out.

Ms. Heartshorn considered that and relented. "You can tell people that she had a family emergency. Her mother is very ill, and she had to go back to her hometown to take care of her for a while."

Amy was shocked. "You made Ms. Weller's mother sick so you could take her place here?"

"I'm giving you a story to tell people." Ms. Heartshorn looked at her watch. "You're very late for class. I'll give you a note so you won't be in trouble."

Amy followed her to the desk, where Ms. Heartshorn wrote out an excuse for her. "Can you fix it so Tasha and I don't have to stay for detention this afternoon?" Amy asked.

The teacher handed her the note. "No. Don't expect any special privileges from me."

As *if.*

Outside the classroom, Amy took a quick look at the note Ms. Heartshorn had given her. The teacher hadn't written down the time, which meant Amy didn't have to run to her class. Instead, she went down to the gym level, where the pay phones were.

Fishing in her bag, she took out a piece of napkin and dialed the number written on it.

"Yes?"

"Uh, Mr. Lasky?"

"Who is this?" the voice asked.

"This is Amy Candler . . . Ms. Weller's student."

The voice became warmer. "Oh yes, of course! How are you, Amy?"

"I'm fine. I know how worried you've been about Ms. Weller, so I thought I'd call with some information."

"You have information?" He sounded very surprised.

"Yes, I found out from another teacher that Ms. Weller's mother is sick. Ms. Weller is taking care of her. Back in her hometown."

"San Diego?"

"What?"

"That's her hometown, San Diego. She isn't there—I called. And her mother is fine."

Amy didn't know what to say. She hadn't considered the possibility that Mr. Lasky might have tried to find Ms. Weller in her hometown. Obviously, Ms. Heartshorn's story wasn't going to placate *him*.

"What's the name of the teacher who told you this story?" he wanted to know.

Amy hesitated. She didn't feel any loyalty toward Ms. Heartshorn, even if she *was* on Amy's side. Even so, she had a pretty good suspicion she shouldn't be spreading her name around.

"Oh, I can't remember. Some teacher . . ."

"It wouldn't happen to be the teacher who's substituting for her, was it?"

Amy winced. "Uh, why would her substitute make up a story about Ms. Weller?"

"I don't know if you're aware of this, Amy, but there's a freeze on teacher hirings. The only way a person can get a job as a teacher is if another teacher leaves. Maybe this substitute arranged to get rid of Bonnie."

"Oh, Mr. Lasky, I don't think Ms. Heartshorn would—" Amy caught herself, but it was too late.

"Heartshorn," he repeated.

"Look, Mr. Lasky, I have to go, I'm late for class. If I hear anything else, I'll call you, okay? Bye!"

Poor man, she thought. He must be really crazy about Ms. Weller to think that another teacher would hurt her just to get her job. She couldn't imagine anyone wanting to be a teacher *that* badly. And what was Mr. Lasky going to do now? Call Ms. Heartshorn and accuse her of something?

Amy smiled. After the way Ms. Heartshorn had been treating her, she *deserved* it.

n9e

When her mother walked in the door that evening, Amy was with Tasha and Eric, but she didn't let that stop her from confronting Nancy with a disapproving look. "Mom, I can't believe you knew all about Ms. Heartshorn and you didn't tell me."

"How about giving me a chance to take off my coat before you start yelling?" Nancy asked. "Well, at least now you know why I wasn't taking your complaints about the substitute seriously."

"But why was it such a big secret?" Tasha asked.

"Yeah, we all knew about Mr. Devon," Eric added.

"Maybe Ms. Heartshorn doesn't want to end up like Mr. Devon," Nancy pointed out.

That shut them up for a moment.

"What Ms. Heartshorn told me," Nancy continued, "was that she thought it would be easier to observe Amy if Amy didn't know she was being observed. You guys want something to eat? I picked up a treat."

They all followed her into the kitchen. "Where do these people like Devon and Heartshorn come from, anyway?" Eric asked. "Is there some sort of clone protection agency?"

"I can't tell you, Eric," Nancy said. She opened a bakery box and began placing cupcakes on a platter.

"Sure you can, you can trust us!" he protested.

She smiled. "I know I can trust you kids. But when I say I can't tell you, I honestly mean I don't know. You have to remember, I was a young woman when I worked on Project Crescent, and I wasn't in a very high position. There's a lot that Dr. Jaleski didn't share with the younger scientists. To protect us. But just as I knew you could trust Mr. Devon, Amy, I know you can trust Ms. Heartshorn." She put the tray of cupcakes on the kitchen table and went to the sink to fill the teakettle.

"I still don't see why I need a caretaker," Amy complained, taking a cupcake. "It's not like I've been running around acting like Wonder Woman."

"It's the e-mails," Tasha said decisively. "I told you, you have be careful about what you say when you write to Andy every day." It was less than a fraction of a second before she realized whose name she'd just uttered. "Oh no."

Amy's stomach was churning as she watched Eric's reaction. His cupcake froze in midair. Then, abruptly, he put it back on the platter and got up.

"Are you leaving, Eric?" Amy's mother asked. "You haven't eaten anything."

"I'm not hungry," he said.

She looked at him in disbelief.

"And I just remembered something I have to do." Without even saying goodbye, he left.

"I'm sorry!" Tasha said.

Amy sighed. "That's okay. He'd find out sooner or later."

Later that evening, lying in bed, she thought about Eric. She couldn't really blame him for his jealousy. She herself had been jealous in the past, when she thought Eric was interested in another girl. Even so, she knew her situation was different. She felt sure that she loved Eric. But the bond she had with Andy went beyond romance. He understood her in a way Eric never could.

She kept glancing across the room at her computer. With Ms. Heartshorn's warnings in her head, she'd resisted checking her mailbox. But it was almost as if she could hear Andy's e-mail, calling "Read me, read me!" Maybe she could just log on and check her box. She wouldn't have to answer Andy's e-mail. That should satisfy Ms. Heartshorn.

But when she checked, her e-mail box was empty. This would be the first day Andy had missed since she left Paris. She supposed it had to happen eventually. Once a day would turn into once a week, then once a month.

Unless there was another reason why he hadn't written that day. His computer could be broken. Or he could be away. Or maybe . . . He could be in trouble . . . trapped in a cage, miles below the streets of Paris . . . okay, maybe she was letting her imagination run wild. But she knew she wouldn't be able to sleep that night unless she tried to make contact.

She hesitated, her long purple fingernails hovering over the keys. Then she shoved Ms. Heartshorn's warnings to the back of her mind and started to type.

Hi! Is everything ok? I've got this new teacher, Ms. Heart-shorn, who says she's taking Mr. Devon's place. She's very weird and I don't know how we'll get along. Write when you can. Love, A.

Impulsively she added a row of *x*'s for kisses. Then she clicked on Send Now before she could have second thoughts.

When Tasha came by for her the next morning, Eric wasn't with her. "He's really mad, huh?" Amy asked.

"I guess," Tasha replied.

"Darn. Just when he'd started talking to me again."

Tasha brushed it off. "He'll get over it. Just don't open your e-mail window and send any more messages to you know who."

Amy grinned. "I already did."

"Amy! Are you nuts? Ms. Heartshorn told you to stay off the Internet."

"I'm sure she just wants me to be careful about what I write, that's all. I'm going to talk to her today. If she's really on my side, we're going to have to get along."

But that wasn't going to be easy. When she walked into homeroom, Amy greeted Ms. Heartshorn with a cheerful "Good morning" and a big smile. The teacher didn't even look up. Amy took her seat.

"Ooh, I love your nail polish," Claire Dudley said.

Now Ms. Heartshorn looked up. "Amy, Claire, no talking." And Amy hadn't even opened her mouth!

Just after the bell rang, before the morning announcements, the classroom door opened and a boy came in wheeling a cart that held big boxes. "Supplies from the office," he announced.

"Put them in the storage cabinet," Ms. Heartshorn directed him.

The boy lifted a box and staggered under the weight of it. He looked like he was about to drop it, and Amy jumped up. "I'll help you," she said, and grabbed the box before it could fall.

"Wow, you're strong," the boy remarked.

"Amy, take your seat!" Ms. Heartshorn practically screamed.

Amy couldn't really blame her for being annoyed. This was the kind of thing she shouldn't do, show off her strength. It had been a spontaneous gesture, and she wanted the teacher to know she hadn't done it on purpose. As soon as homeroom was over, she went to Ms. Heartshorn's desk, where the teacher was marking papers.

"I'm sorry, I forgot, I won't do that again," she promised. When Ms. Heartshorn didn't respond, Amy asked, "Are you mad at me?"

The teacher put the pen down and looked at her. "Amy, I am here on a job. I don't get 'mad,' as you put it. I don't bring that kind of feeling to my work."

Amy gazed at her curiously. "Ms. Heartshorn, can I ask you something?"

The teacher was barely able to contain the impatience in her voice. "What do you want, Amy?"

"Did you ever know Mr. Devon?"

"I may have met him once."

"He was nice," Amy said. "He saved my life once. I remember, when I first met him, he was—"

Ms. Heartshorn broke in. "Amy, I don't have time to listen to your reminiscences now."

No, it would definitely not be easy developing a friendly relationship with this woman. "But I'm not going to give up," Amy told Tasha at lunch.

"Yeah, okay," Tasha murmured.

"And I don't believe her when she says she has no feelings about her work. Do you?"

"Mm."

"You do?"

Tasha blinked. "Huh?"

Amy looked at her in annoyance. "I don't think you've heard one thing I've said! What's the matter with you?"

"Nothing," Tasha said unconvincingly.

"Well, anyway," Amy continued, "I'm going to try to talk to her again after school today. Can you wait for me?"

"No, I've got something to do," Tasha said.

"What?" Amy asked.

"Just something." Tasha looked extremely uncomfortable. Amy couldn't get anything more out of her. Tasha kept looking at her watch. Then, only ten minutes after they'd sat down, she announced, "Oh, I have to go."

"Where?"

But Tasha was already gone. It was strange—she was acting almost like her brother.

Amy cornered Eric that afternoon by his locker. "Is something wrong with Tasha?" she demanded.

"Huh? No." He turned away from her and began opening his locker.

"Eric, listen to me, I know you're mad that I'm writing to Andy, but it doesn't mean anything, we're just friends, and—"

"I'm not mad," Eric said.

"You're not?"

He wouldn't meet her eyes. "I gotta go." He took off. Amy gazed after him in bewilderment. What was wrong with everyone today? And now she had to deal with Ms. Heartshorn.

The teacher was at her desk, still marking papers. Amy considered telling her that if she didn't assign so many essays to write she wouldn't have to do so much grading, but she didn't think Ms. Heartshorn would appreciate the suggestion.

She rapped on the open door.

"Yes?"

"I was wondering if I could talk to you for a minute," Amy said. "If you're not too busy."

The teacher put the pen down. "Is there a problem?"

"Not a problem, exactly." Amy came in and stood beside the desk. She waited for Ms. Heartshorn to give her an encouraging nod or word, but when it didn't happen she plunged in anyway. "See, Ms. Heartshorn, I know you think I'm a pain, but I have to tell you, it's not easy, you know?"

"What's not easy?"

"Being me! I mean, don't get me wrong, I like myself, I like being special. But sometimes I wish I could be like everyone else. Does that make sense?"

"Amy, where is this going? What's your point?"

"I'm just trying to tell you where I'm coming from. I thought it might help."

"Help? Help what?"

"Help you to understand me!" Amy cried out in desperation. "So you'll like me!"

"I don't need to like you, Amy," Ms. Heartshorn said. "I am not here to be your friend. I'm here to watch out for you, that's all. Now, do you have anything relevant to tell me?"

Amy couldn't speak. Ms. Heartshorn misunderstood the silence.

"Relevant," the teacher repeated. "That means relating to the matter at hand. Pertinent. To the point."

"I *know* what 'relevant' means," Amy retorted. "I've got a genetically engineered brain, remember? And for your information, I'm also a human being!"

With as much dignity as she could muster, she stomped out of the room. She was seething all the way home. And this was her mother's late day teaching at the university—she wouldn't be there to listen to Amy moan.

As soon as Amy walked into the house, she went to the phone and dialed Tasha's number. Eric answered.

"Hi, it's me. Oh, Eric, I just tried to talk to Ms. Heartshorn again. You wouldn't believe what she said."

"Uh, listen, Amy, I'm sorry, but I'm off to basketball practice, and I have to leave right this minute."

"Oh. Well, put Tasha on, okay?"

"She's real busy. I'll tell her to call you back, okay? Bye." And he actually hung up on her.

Amy looked at the phone in disbelief. This was the last put-down she'd put up with. She ran outside and across the lawn.

Mrs. Morgan answered the door. "Hi, Amy. Tasha's in her room."

"Thanks." Amy ran up the stairs and burst into Tasha's bedroom. She found her best friend lying on her bed, flipping through a magazine.

"You don't look so busy to me," Amy accused.

Tasha looked up, and there was no mistaking the guilty expression on her face. Then the door of Eric's room opened and he came out. Barefoot, in ripped jeans, he was clearly not on his way to play basketball.

"What's going on?" Amy demanded.

Tasha looked past her at Eric. "See, I told you this wouldn't work."

"*What* wouldn't work?" Amy practically shrieked.

"We both got notes during first period today," Tasha told her. "From Ms. Heartshorn. She wanted to see us."

"You and Eric?"

"Yeah," Eric said. "She told us we shouldn't spend so much time with you. And we shouldn't let you tell us personal stuff."

"Because we're not supposed to know about you," Tasha continued. "She said you have to learn to deal with things on your own. I told her I was your best friend, and she said people like you couldn't have best friends."

"She said if we really cared about you," Eric said, "we would cut you out of our lives."

"And you believed her?" Amy asked.

"She was pretty convincing," Eric said.

Then Tasha burst into tears. "I knew I couldn't do it. I told her I couldn't do it. But she said I had to try, that it was for your own good."

By now Amy was shaking. "I can't believe it. I can't believe it! She's crazy. She's evil. I hate her!" Now Amy was crying too. Eric was the only one whose eyes were dry, but at least he looked seriously depressed.

Tasha wiped her tears away. "Amy, are you *sure* she's on your side? Mr. Devon wasn't the friendliest person in the world, but at least he wasn't mean."

"Yeah," Eric said. "Maybe she's, you know, one of *them.* From the organization."

Amy shook her head. "My mom trusts her. And you know my mom, she's usually suspicious of everyone. I'm just going to have to put up with Ms. Heartshorn."

When she went back home, the phone was ringing. It was her mother. "Hi, honey, is everything okay?" Nancy asked.

Amy tried to sound more cheerful than she felt. "Yeah, everything's okay."

"I'm running a little late, I had a meeting after class, but I'll pick up some dinner on the way home."

"Okay. See you later." Amy hung up and mentally congratulated herself on not even having mentioned Ms. Heartshorn. Then the phone rang again.

"Hello?"

"Is this Amy?"

"Yes."

"Amy, this is Dan Lasky."

"Hi, Mr. Lasky. Have you heard from Ms. Weller?"

"Not a word," he said. "But I can't stop thinking about that woman who's substituting for her."

"Ms. Heartshorn?"

"Yes. You know, people will go to great lengths to get a job these days. I'm still wondering if she knows more about Bonnie's disappearance than she's letting on. In fact, I've been thinking about hiring a private investigator to look into her. I want to know if she has a criminal background."

Personally, Amy thought that sounded a little far-fetched. But the idea of Ms. Heartshorn getting followed and maybe even hassled wasn't entirely unappealing. "I guess that's not a bad idea," she said.

"I'll let you know what I find out," he promised.

Hanging up, Amy realized that it had been pretty stupid of her to encourage him. An investigation might not only reveal stuff about Ms. Heartshorn; it might reveal things about Amy—things that shouldn't be known. Well, it was too late to do anything about that now.

She was distracted by a sound coming from her mother's office off the kitchen. She looked inside and saw a sheet of paper emerging from her mother's fax machine. She went in and picked it up.

It was from Andy! She'd given him her mother's fax number because he was going to send her some photos from their time together in Paris.

This wasn't a photograph, though. It was a drawing— a big heart with a line through it like an arrow. Except it wasn't an arrow, just a diagonal line. And looking more closely, Amy could see a faint diagonal line running in the other direction. It was like an X across the heart.

It was weird. There were no words on the sheet. Was this a discreet message? Was he saying something like "I'm not your valentine"? "I don't love you"? It wasn't even Valentine's Day, and he'd never said he *did* love her, so why would he now say that he didn't?

It didn't make any sense. She stared at the drawing for a while and tried to come up with another meaning. Heart, heart . . . Heartshorn? And the *X* . . . She sucked in her breath. She'd just written Andy about Ms. Heartshorn yesterday. Could it be that Andy knew something about her? Was he trying, without words, to tell Amy what he knew?

Like don't trust Ms. Heartshorn?

ten 10

Amy was in English class the next day when she saw Mr. Lasky. Ms. Heartshorn had instructed the students to read the next chapter in *Huckleberry Finn*. Naturally Amy finished the chapter in minutes, but mindful of Ms. Heartshorn's warning about calling attention to herself, she sat there with the open book in front of her and pretended to still be reading.

Eventually her eyes drifted away from the words she'd read over and over, and she found herself looking at the ceiling, at the back of someone's head, out the window into the parking lot. She was in the process of counting the red cars when another red car entered the lot.

She watched without much interest as it pulled into one of the parking spaces. But her interest level rose dramatically when she saw the car door open and Mr. Lasky got out. He stood there in the parking lot and looked around. Even from this distance, Amy could see that he was uncertain and excited.

She got up and went to Ms. Heartshorn's desk. "Can I be excused to go to the rest room?"

Without expression, the teacher took a rest room pass out of the desk drawer and handed it to Amy. When Amy walked out into the hall, there was no one around, so she went into double speed and moved swiftly to the exit.

Mr. Lasky was still standing in the parking lot, as if waiting for someone. Relief swept over his face when he saw Amy. "Amy, thank goodness! I didn't know where to go."

But even in his relief, she could see that he was still upset. "What's wrong? Why are you here?"

"I had a phone call this morning. Bonnie's been kidnapped, and she's being held for ransom."

"Kidnapped!" Amy echoed. Of all the possibilities in the world, that was the last one that would have occurred to her. Who would kidnap a teacher? It wasn't like they had lots of money or power or fame. She thought hard. "Did the caller say why she was kidnapped? Maybe he's an old boyfriend or something."

"No, it was a woman's voice. And she didn't say why Bonnie had been taken. She's demanding a million dollars for Bonnie's safe return."

"Wow!" It was all Amy could think of to say. This was so confusing. "But why did this woman call *you*? It's not like you're Ms. Weller's husband. Why didn't she call Ms. Weller's family in San Diego?"

"Who knows? I don't even know how she got my name!"

"Did you go to the police?"

"No. She said if I contacted the police, I'd never see Bonnie alive again."

Amy didn't know what to think. On the one hand, this was incredibly frightening news. On the other hand, it was almost too bizarre to be believable.

"Excuse me for asking this," Amy said, "but are you a millionaire? Maybe the woman saw the two of you together and thought you were, I don't know, engaged to be married or something."

"I'm no millionaire," Mr. Lasky assured her. "Not even close."

"Well, I don't think Ms. Weller is rich," Amy said.

"No, she's not rich," Mr. Lasky said. "She certainly

doesn't have a million dollars lying around. And neither does her family."

Amy was utterly bewildered. None of this made any sense at all. "What are you supposed to do now? Get the money and deliver it somewhere?"

Mr. Lasky didn't have the opportunity to answer her. From behind Amy, footsteps approached and a harsh voice called out.

"Amy Candler! You're not supposed to be out here. Get back to class this minute!"

"Yes, Ms. Heartshorn," Amy said. She looked at Mr. Lasky to see if he was showing any reaction to the name. He was staring at the teacher. For a brief moment Ms. Heartshorn stared right back at him. Then she motioned for Amy to follow her back into the building. Amy only had enough time to give Mr. Lasky an apologetic shrug, but he didn't notice. His eyes were fixed on Ms. Heartshorn.

After the last class of the day, Amy reported Mr. Lasky's news to Tasha. Tasha wasn't terribly alarmed, and she quickly came up with an opinion as to what it was all about. "It was a prank," she announced firmly. "Some kid here at school called him."

"But how would anyone here know about Ms. Weller and Mr. Lasky?" Amy wondered. The girls were walking out the main entrance. They stopped on the school steps.

"*We* knew about them," Tasha pointed out. "Someone else could have seen them together somewhere."

That was true. "But he said it was the voice of a woman, not a girl," Amy pointed out.

Again Tasha had an answer. "Lots of girls can sound older. You know Simone Cusack. When she wants to skip school, she calls the office and says she's her own mother. She makes her voice deeper, and she tells the secretary that Simone is sick and won't be in school. The secretary believes her. Then, when the absent notices get to the office, the secretary doesn't bother to call Simone's home to check on her."

"I wonder if I could get away with that," Amy mused. She lowered her voice. "Hello, this is Nancy Candler."

"Forget it," Tasha told her. "But I'm not accusing Simone. Lots of kids can change their voices."

Amy had an idea. "Maybe we should check out the girls who are in the drama club."

"Yeah," Tasha agreed. "I can get a list of drama club members from the *Parkside News* office. We can start calling them as soon as we get home. Maybe I can get Eric to help us."

For the first time in ages, Eric actually met them to walk home together, so Amy was able to tell him all the news. She and Tasha had just started to explain their plan to him, and the three of them were almost out of the parking lot, when the red car Amy had seen earlier pulled in. Mr. Lasky jumped out.

"Amy! I'm glad I caught you!" His face was flushed and he looked even more excited than he had earlier. But he stopped talking when he saw Tasha and Eric. "Could you take a little ride with me?" he asked Amy. "I need to speak to you alone for a moment."

"Tasha and Eric know everything," Amy told him. "You can talk in front of them."

He frowned, but he recovered quickly. "Okay. When I was here earlier and that teacher came out and spoke to you, something clicked. I knew that voice. I recognized it."

Amy gasped. "You mean—"

He nodded. "That was the woman who called and said she'd kidnapped Bonnie Weller."

Amy clapped a hand to her mouth. Tasha and Eric looked stunned too. "Are you sure?" Eric asked. "People don't always sound the same over the phone as they do in real life."

"I have a very high-tech digital phone," Mr. Lasky told him. "The sound quality is excellent. Besides, now

I have proof." He turned to Amy. "Remember I told you I was going to hire a private investigator to look into Ms. Heartshorn? Well, he was able to get a log of all phone calls made from her number. And at the exact time that I received the ransom call, a call was made from her home to mine."

Amy sucked in her breath. It sounded like he was definitely on to something. "I *knew* she was evil," she said. "I *knew* it."

Mr. Lasky continued. "The investigator searched Heartshorn's apartment, but Bonnie wasn't there. She's probably tied up in some nasty rat-infested basement somewhere." His eyes filled with tears. "He's got a whole team searching for her now."

"Did he find any clues in the apartment?" Tasha asked.

"Well, there was this." He reached into his pocket and pulled out a road map. "It's a map of southern Oregon. And there's an *x* on this highway," he said, pointing. "The investigator's sending someone to check it out and see if that's where Bonnie's being held."

Amy gazed at the map. Then she looked at Eric. She could see that he recognized it too.

"Ohmigod," Tasha said. "That's where Wilderness Adventure took us camping!" She looked at Amy. "Isn't that where Mr. Devon was—"

Amy pinched her. Tasha yelped and shot her a dirty

look, but at least she shut up. Amy didn't want to have to explain who Mr. Devon was to Mr. Lasky.

"Does this mean something to you?" Mr. Lasky asked. He was looking at Amy with so much anxiety and intensity, it made her uncomfortable. She hastened to stop him from pursuing a false lead.

"It's just a place we went camping once, that's all," she told him. "I'm sure it's just a coincidence."

He didn't look convinced. "I don't believe in coincidences. I'm going to have the area checked out thoroughly." He got back into his car. "I'd better stay by my phone now. I'm expecting another call from your substitute teacher. And if the investigator doesn't find Bonnie in Oregon, I have to dig up a million dollars."

"Call me if you find out anything," Amy told him, and the man nodded before driving out of the lot.

"Well, I guess we don't have to make the calls to the drama club members," Tasha remarked.

Eric scratched his head. "I don't get it. If he's so sure that Heartshorn kidnapped Weller, why doesn't he just go into the school right now and corner her?"

"Because she'd just deny it," Tasha replied. "Then he might never see Ms. Weller alive again. Anyway, he doesn't care about Ms. Heartshorn. He just wants to get Ms. Weller back safe and sound." She sighed. "He must really love her."

There was nothing any of them could do now. And they didn't talk much on their way home. Everyone seemed to be lost in their own thoughts. Amy was still trying to make some sense out of this crazy business. She knew that Tasha was contemplating the great love Mr. Lasky was showing for Ms. Weller. She had no idea what Eric was thinking about.

If she herself was kidnapped, would Eric go crazy trying to come up with a million dollars to ransom her? In a way, by keeping up her relationship with Andy, she was doing Eric a big favor. They could split the cost of her ransom and only have to come up with half a million each.

Because it was sweeps week, *Crimesolvers* was on that evening as well as the next night, and this time Eric and Tasha were coming to her place. Her mother very kindly provided huge bags of taco chips and homemade salsa for dipping.

"Mom, you want to watch with us?" Amy asked, but she was only being polite. She knew what her mother's answer would be.

"No thanks, kids, it's too gruesome for me. I'll be in my office." Nancy disappeared back inside the kitchen.

The show wasn't quite as exciting as usual that evening. There was a babies-switched-at-birth situation that got resolved easily, and another report on Canadian drug smuggling. There was also an update on the Green Spiders trial.

"Closing arguments have been made, and the jurors are now deliberating," Roger Graves reported. "Security around the Los Angeles hotel where the jury is sequestered has been tightened. It is believed that several attempts have been made to identify members of the jury on behalf of the Green Spiders. They're trying to create a climate of fear that will discourage the jurors from reaching a verdict of 'guilty.' A bellhop has been arrested for bringing a video camera into the hotel. He is suspected of having taken a bribe from a Green Spiders member to tape the jury deliberations."

"It must be so scary to be on that jury," Tasha commented. "Those Green Spiders are vicious. If they find out—"

"Shhh!" Eric hissed. The host had moved on to something else.

"Last week we told you about a mysterious killing that occurred on a highway in southern Oregon. A man by the name of Devon was discovered behind the wheel of his car. He was dead. Up until now, police have been unable to ascertain the means by which he was murdered, and there have been no leads as to the perpetrator of the crime. But thanks to you, they now have something to go on. A viewer who happened to be driving down that highway at the time has notified us that a person was seen leaving the scene of the crime. This viewer has met with our resident sketch artist, and together they have come up with a portrait of the suspect."

A black-and-white drawing appeared on the screen.

"If you or anyone you know has any knowledge as to the identity of this person, please call us immediately here at *Crimesolvers*. Any information will be kept confidential."

Amy stared at the screen. Was she seeing what she thought she was seeing? When she was finally able to tear her gaze away, she saw that Tasha's and Eric's eyes were glued to the screen too. All three of them recognized the portrait. And in unison, they all whispered the name.

"Ms. Heartshorn!"

eleven

Ms. Heartshorn.

There was no question about it. The woman's face was clearly recognizable. Then it disappeared and a commercial took its place.

Tasha recovered first. "Maybe . . . maybe she was working with Mr. Devon, and that's why she was in Oregon."

"No," Amy replied. "She barely knew Mr. Devon." It all started to come together. "You know what, guys? This explains everything."

"Then explain it to me," Eric said. "Because I'm totally confused."

"It explains why I couldn't relate to her," Amy said. "Because she's not Mr. Devon's replacement. She's one of *them*."

"The organization," Tasha said in a hushed voice.

"Exactly." Amy began to pace the room. "Okay, this is the way I'm seeing it. Mr. Lasky was right. Ms. Heartshorn arranged to make Ms. Weller disappear so she could take her place, so she could watch me."

"Why did she have to make Ms. Weller disappear?" Eric asked. "Couldn't she have just taken a job at Parkside?"

"There's been a freeze on hiring," Tasha told him. "The only way she could work there was if another teacher left."

Amy continued. "All this time, she's been testing me, trying to figure out exactly what my skills are. That's why she let me go ahead and try out for cheerleading. And she told you to stay away from me because she didn't want you to interfere."

"Interfere with what?" Eric asked.

"With—with whatever she's planning to do to me." The full impact of this thought made Amy shudder. "I mean, do you realize what her plans could be? If she *killed* Mr. Devon, she's ruthless. She's capable of doing anything!"

"Do you think she's killed Ms. Weller?" Tasha wondered aloud.

"I don't know." Amy went to the phone. "I'm going to call Mr. Lasky right now and tell him what we saw. If Ms. Weller's still alive, we have to find her. Now."

"*We?*" Tasha asked weakly, but Amy was already dialing. More pieces of the puzzle had fallen into place. The crossed-out heart from Andy was a not-so-subtle warning. The road map of Oregon in Ms. Heartshorn's apartment had guilt written all over it.

One thing still puzzled Amy, though. Somehow Ms. Heartshorn had convinced Nancy Candler that she was on the right side. Amy's mother wasn't usually that gullible.

She heard the phone ringing twice, and then there was a clicking sound.

"Hello, Mr. Lasky?" Amy began, but she stopped when she realized she was hearing a recorded voice.

"The number you have dialed is no longer in service. Please verify the number and try again."

Amy frowned. Could she have misdialed? She tried again. When the same recording started, she hung up. "His phone's out of order," she announced.

"Maybe we should just call the police and tell them what we know," Tasha suggested.

Amy shook her head. "They'll ask too many questions. We'll have to go find Mr. Lasky."

She picked up the phone book and began thumbing through it. "Lasky, Lasky . . ." She found a D. Lasky whose phone number corresponded with the one she'd been dialing and noted the address. Mentally she conjured up a map of Los Angeles. It wasn't anywhere near where they lived.

But they could find a taxi on a nearby avenue. And if Tasha and Eric were willing to chip in with her, they could probably get enough money pulled together to pay for it.

There was still one more problem to deal with. Nancy Candler.

The object of Amy's concern came into the living room carrying a platter of chocolate-colored squares. "Who wants brownies?" she asked.

"I'll pass, thanks," Eric answered. "But I'd love some ice cream."

"I'm sorry, Eric," Nancy said. "We don't have any ice cream. But the brownies are delicious."

"I'm craving ice cream," Eric insisted. "Let's go to Bailey's."

"Bailey's?" Nancy echoed.

Amy saw what Eric was doing. "It's that new ice cream place, over by school," she told her mother.

"Oh, honey, I don't feel like going out now. I've got a cold coming on, and I think I should go straight to bed."

"We can walk to Bailey's," Eric said.

Nancy's forehead puckered. "Now? It's dark out."

Eric pulled himself up straighter. "Ms. Candler, I'm fourteen, I can take care of Amy and Tasha."

Amy resisted the urge to kick him. He knew very well that Amy was more likely to end up taking care of *him*.

But somehow he managed to convince Nancy Candler. And they were free. "That was quick thinking, Eric," Amy told him with approval.

He preened. "Yeah, it was like something a clone would think up, right?"

"Absolutely," Amy assured him, and she resisted an urge to give him a hug. He'd only have been embarrassed.

Pooling their money, they came up with enough for a taxi to Mr. Lasky's address. It turned out to be in a small complex of shabby-looking apartments, and Amy was a little surprised. She couldn't imagine Ms. Weller hanging out in a place like this.

"I wonder why he lives in such a crummy place," she said.

"Maybe he's saving his money to buy Ms. Weller a gigantic diamond engagement ring," Tasha suggested.

135

She was such a romantic. Amy only hoped Ms. Weller was still in a condition to wear an engagement ring.

They found the mailboxes, which gave them Mr. Lasky's apartment number, and they climbed the stairs that led to the second level. Amy knocked on his door.

Mr. Lasky didn't seem all that surprised to see them, and they soon found out why. "You saw *Crimesolvers!*" he exclaimed. "And my private investigator just called. He found out where Bonnie is being held! I'm going there right now."

"We'll come with you," Amy said excitedly.

Tasha wasn't quite as enthusiastic. "This could be dangerous."

"Only Heartshorn is there with her," Mr. Lasky said. "And the investigator is meeting us with a couple of his agents. We can take Heartshorn on."

Amy relished the thought of attacking Ms. Heartshorn, pinning her to the ground, giving her a couple of punches and maybe even tying her up. Not to mention the idea of rescuing Ms. Weller. "Let's go!"

They all piled into Mr. Lasky's red car and took off. "Where is Ms. Weller?" Eric asked.

"She's being held in an office building at Sunshine Square," Mr. Lasky told them.

"We know Sunshine Square!" Tasha exclaimed.

"That's the mall with the sports arena where Amy and I used to take gymnastics."

Amy remembered. And as they approached the mall, she remembered the office building, too. The memory made her shudder. She'd once been sent to see a dentist in that building, way back before she knew that her teeth were so perfect they would never require the services of a dentist.

The dentist had turned out to be someone associated with the organization. He'd tried to get X rays of Amy's teeth to ascertain her identity, and he'd tried to knock her out with nitrous oxide, the gas some dentists used to help patients relax. Amy had just barely escaped.

It made perfect sense that Ms. Weller was being held captive in the same building. Obviously, this was one of the organization's regular places. Maybe even their L.A. headquarters.

But something else was going on at Sunshine Square that night. As Mr. Lasky turned to enter the parking lot, they saw that it was blocked. Some sort of traveling carnival had been set up, and there were crowds of people milling about. Mr. Lasky turned the car around and found a place to leave it on a side street. They all jumped out and walked hurriedly toward the office building.

It wasn't easy dodging the meandering groups with their cotton candy and getting around the game booths and rides that had been set up. Finally they reached the office building on the other side of the mall.

It looked dark and deserted. But just as they were walking toward the entrance, the door opened. Lucky for them, the person coming out had her back to them. But they all recognized her easily.

Ms. Heartshorn was moving purposefully into the lot. Mr. Lasky stared after her. "I want to know where she's going," he said.

"But Ms. Weller is supposed to be in this building," Amy pointed out. "Shouldn't we go see if she's okay first?"

"You're right," Mr. Lasky said. He turned to Eric and Tasha. "You two, follow Heartshorn. Amy and I will find Bonnie. Meet us back here."

"Right," Eric said. He grabbed Tasha's arm and they took off. Amy followed Mr. Lasky into the building. All the office doors were closed. It was completely silent.

"Do you know what office she's being held in?" Amy asked.

"The investigator said it's on the third floor," Mr. Lasky told her. They took the stairs and came out into what appeared to be another silent and deserted hallway. Amy looked around uneasily.

"It looks like we got here before the investigator and his agents," she said. But Mr. Lasky didn't seem concerned about this. He strode on ahead, looking at the numbers on the office doors. When he got to number 308, he paused. "This is it," he said.

The sign on the door read ROBERT GREENE, D.D.S., and Amy's stomach turned over. This was the office she'd been in before. She steeled herself for the blast of an unpleasant memory that would hit her as soon as they went inside.

The reception area was exactly the way she remembered it—a desk, a small sofa, a table with magazines. But no receptionist. And no Ms. Weller, either. Mr. Lasky looked around.

Amy pointed to a door. "There's an examining room through there," she whispered.

Mr. Lasky nodded. "You wait here," he instructed her. He went to the door, opened it, and went in. Just as the door closed behind him, the main office door opened. Amy spun around and faced the substitute teacher.

"Get out of here!" Ms. Heartshorn said through her teeth. But Amy was no longer taking orders from her. She leaped forward, moving so fast that Heartshorn had no time to react. It was almost too easy, delivering one sharp precise punch to the substitute's head. Amy stepped back to watch in satisfaction as the woman crumpled into an unconscious heap at her feet.

At the same time, she heard Mr. Lasky calling to her excitedly. She started into the corridor that led to the examining office. At that very second, an odd thought occurred to her.

When she had tried to call Mr. Lasky from home, the recording had told her the phone was out of order. Yet when they arrived at Mr. Lasky's, he told them he'd just been talking to the investigator on the phone. Maybe he had two separate lines. Or a mobile phone.

She had no further opportunity to consider the possible explanations. Because at that very moment, a mask was pressed against her face. A sweet, vaguely familiar scent came over her. Her memory began to rewind, and suddenly it was almost a year earlier and she was in this same office, with the big chair and the metal instruments and the tank on the floor.

The smell of nitrous oxide filled her nose. And then . . . nothing.

twelve 12

When she came to, Amy had no idea how long she'd been unconscious. All she knew was that her arms were tied together behind her back and her entire body was bound to the chair on which she was sitting.

Directly across the room, a grim-faced Ms. Heart-shorn sat bound to another chair. She was awake, and her expression was even more sour than usual.

"Well, it's about time," she snapped at Amy. "You should have enough strength to break your ropes. Then you can untie me."

Amy just stared at her.

"That wasn't very intelligent, Amy," Ms. Heartshorn

continued. "Hitting me like that. I could have prevented Lasky from knocking you out."

Now Amy was wondering if the nitrous oxide had permanently affected her hearing. She busied herself, concentrating all her strength on her bound wrists. With some effort, she was finally able to break the rope. Then she proceeded to free the rest of her body.

"Now, untie me," Ms. Heartshorn commanded.

Amy got up and stretched. "Not so fast," she said. "I want some explanations."

Ms. Heartshorn scowled. "You haven't figured it out yet? Perhaps you're not as intelligent as we give you credit for being."

"We?" Amy said. "You mean the organization?"

"No," the substitute replied. "I mean Project Crescent."

Amy glared at her. "I saw your picture on *Crimesolvers*. You killed Mr. Devon."

Ms. Heartshorn rolled her eyes. "You silly girl. How do you think that picture got on TV?"

"A witness—" Amy began.

Ms. Heartshorn shook her head. "It was Lasky. He contacted *Crimesolvers*."

Amy looked at her doubtfully. Ms. Heartshorn let out an exaggerated sigh of impatience.

"Listen carefully, because I'm only going to tell you

this once. Lasky is with the organization. He established a relationship with Ms. Weller so he could make contact with you. He tried to distract you by turning you against me. Apparently he succeeded."

"I didn't need Lasky to turn me against you," Amy shot back. "You accomplished that all by yourself."

Ms. Heartshorn let out another exasperated sigh. "You really must learn not to take everything so personally, Amy. Project Crescent is bigger than your silly little emotional needs."

"There *is* no Project Crescent," Amy countered. "Not anymore. My mother told me all evidence was destroyed twelve years ago."

"Your mother may not know everything," Ms. Heartshorn replied.

"Where is Ms. Weller?" Amy wanted to know.

"I haven't the slightest idea," Ms. Heartshorn answered. "All I know is that she is alive and well. But that's irrelevant at this point in time. What's significant now is the fact that you allowed Lasky to escape. With some very real evidence."

"What real evidence?" Amy demanded. "He obviously didn't take me with him."

"How could he take you away? There are hundreds of people outside attending a carnival. He couldn't walk out of this building dragging an unconscious girl."

"So he doesn't have any evidence," Amy said. "Because he doesn't have me."

"He doesn't need *you*. Only a part of you. Something that can be used to extract DNA."

Amy's insides began to flip-flop, and she put a hand to her head. "What did he take? A piece of hair?"

"No," Ms. Heartshorn said somberly. "He cut off your fingernails."

Amy looked at her hands. Her long purple nails were indeed practically gone, leaving only stubby, crooked bits behind. And she started to laugh.

"What's the matter?" Ms. Heartshorn almost shrieked. "Have you lost your mind? Do you realize how serious this is?"

By now Amy was laughing so hard, the tears were streaming from her eyes. She was barely able to choke out the explanation. "My nails—they were fakes!"

Ms. Heartshorn faltered. "What?"

"What Lasky has isn't going to reveal a lot of genetic information. How much DNA can you get from ten pieces of plastic?"

Ms. Heartshorn's mouth fell open, and she sat speechless. Finally Amy decided she could be trusted. Still laughing, she untied the woman's arms and legs and released her.

Ms. Heartshorn stood up a little shakily. She started

rubbing the rope marks on one wrist with her other hand.

At that moment the door burst open. Tasha and Eric came running in. Together they made flying leaps, attacking Ms. Heartshorn and pushing her to the floor. Eric held her arms down while Tasha straddled her legs and Ms. Heartshorn struggled.

"Let me go, you fools! Let me go! Amy, tell them the truth!"

Amy couldn't resist taking her time about it. After the way Ms. Heartshorn had treated her for the past couple of weeks, she deserved to suffer a little.

"Amy!"

"Okay, okay." Amy relented and told Eric and Tasha to let the teacher go. It wasn't much revenge . . . but it was definitely sweet.

thirteen 13

When Amy appeared at the breakfast table the next morning, her mother was blowing her nose. "This cold is a misery," she croaked. "I slept for ten hours and it's not any better."

"I can stay home and take care of you," Amy suggested.

Nancy managed a small smile. "Thanks, but I'll be fine. I know you have plans with Tasha and Eric today. Say, what time did you kids get back from the ice cream place last night? I fell asleep just after you left. I hope you weren't out too late."

Amy crossed her fingers behind her back. "Not too

late," she murmured. It wasn't really a lie. After all, late was a relative word. Some people wouldn't consider midnight late at all.

Ms. Heartshorn had actually been human enough to drive them all home. Of course, she'd used the opportunity to lecture them about their foolish and dangerous behavior. And Amy was all too aware that Ms. Heartshorn's attitude toward *her* in the classroom wasn't going to improve after this episode. But at that moment, they were all giddy with relief and laughing over the benefits of fake fingernails.

After breakfast Amy went back to her room to get ready. When she returned downstairs, her mother was curled up on the sofa, watching television. Amy blew her a kiss goodbye and had almost reached the door when an announcement on TV caught her attention.

"We interrupt this program for some late-breaking news. A verdict has been declared in the so-called Green Spiders trial. All the defendants have been found guilty of first-degree murder. The jury has issued a statement that they are proud of their verdict and that they are going public with their identities. The forewoman has agreed to speak to the media."

"We were unanimous in our verdict," a voice declared. "And we refuse to be intimidated by threats from thugs."

It was a very familiar voice. Amy moved alongside her mother so she could see the TV screen. Then she gasped. Not only did she recognize the woman speaking on the news, but the forewoman's name appeared on the screen, too.

Bonnie Weller.

"We're all very happy that this ordeal is finished," Amy's teacher said. "And we look forward to going back to our normal lives. I'm eager to see my students at Parkside Middle School again."

"Yes!" Amy yelled.

"So *that's* how Ms. Heartshorn got her job at Parkside," Nancy Candler remarked. "I wonder what she'll do now."

Amy hoped Ms. Heartshorn would go back to wherever she'd come from. She felt like celebrating. Not only was Ms. Weller alive and well, but with any luck, Amy would never have to see Ms. Heartshorn again. She couldn't wait to tell Tasha and Eric.

The regular TV program had come back on. From back in the kitchen, Amy heard a soft ringing.

"Is that the phone?" her mother asked.

"I think it's your fax machine," Amy said. "I'll go look."

She went to her mother's office and checked the fax tray. A sheet of paper had come through, and at a glance, Amy could see that it was a memo from her mother's university department. A diagonal line was drawn across it.

Amy looked at it for a long time. Then she brought it to her mother. "Mom, why is this memo crossed out?"

Nancy yawned. "Oh, it's nothing, just a problem with the machine. Everything that comes through it gets that line across it." There was a knock on the door. "That must be Tasha and Eric," she murmured.

"I'll see you later—feel better," Amy said cheerfully. So now she knew that what Andy had sent her had nothing to do with Ms. Heartshorn. It was a plain old heart, the symbol of love and romance, and he had sent it to show her how he felt about her.

It was an enormous relief and the answer to the last remaining mystery. But this was one she didn't think she'd share with Eric.

Don't miss

replica

#14
The Beginning

A my is going back to the place where she was born—
Washington, D.C. It's a class trip to take in the historic
sights of the nation's capital. Sure, Amy's uneasy about traveling to the home turf of the people who funded Project
Crescent—the reason she's alive—and is in constant fear of
being captured. But it's a chance to connect with her roots.
After all, what could go wrong?

Well, Amy's mother is a class chaperone, and for her the
trip stirs up memories.

Memories of working in the top-secret government program to develop clones.

Memories of a loved one's battle against a rare genetic
disorder.

Memories of betrayal, and a decision that would forever
change her life.

And now the trip back to where it all began pits mother and
daughter against an enemy both old and new.